P9-CAO-026

A Candlelight Ecstasy Romance®

"WE'D BETTER CHANGE THE SUBJECT BEFORE I START SAYING THINGS AN ENGAGED MAN SHOULDN'T SAY."

"If a man feels like he wants to say 'things' to a woman who's not his fiancée, then maybe he shouldn't be engaged at all," Taryn reminded Reed, reaching out to gently touch his hand. "Can I kiss you?"

"No!" he refused guiltily.

"If I really thought for one minute that you loved Elaine, I wouldn't dream of doing what I'm about to do."

"This is miserable. You're supposed to respect my state of engagement. . . ."

"That's just what your engagement is—a miserable state. How long is it going to take for you to realize it?" Taryn had no idea why she was torturing herself like this; their relationship could never go anywhere. But for the moment it didn't matter. . . .

CANDLELIGHT ECSTASY ROMANCES®

FOREVER AFTER

Lori Copeland

A CANDLELIGHT ECSTASY ROMANCE®

Published by
Dell Publishing Co., Inc.
1 Dag Hammarskjold Plaza
New York, New York 10017

Dell ® TM 681510, Dell Publishing Co., Inc.

Candlelight Ecstasy Romance®, 1,203,540, is a registered
trademark of Dell Publishing Co., Inc., New York, New York.

ISBN: 0-440-12681-9

Printed in the United States of America

First printing—March 1985

In loving memory of my parents, John and Josephine Smart. Their time on earth has passed, but somehow I know they're still watching over me.

To Our Readers:

We have been delighted with your enthusiastic response to Candlelight Ecstasy Romances®, and we thank you for the interest you have shown in this exciting series.

In the upcoming months we will continue to present the distinctive sensuous love stories you have come to expect only from Ecstasy. We look forward to bringing you many more books from your favorite authors and also the very finest work from new authors of contemporary romantic fiction.

As always, we are striving to present the unique, absorbing love stories that you enjoy most—books that are more than ordinary romance. Your suggestions and comments are always welcome. Please write to us at the address below.

Sincerely,

The Editors
Candlelight Romances
1 Dag Hammarskjold Plaza
New York, New York 10017

CHAPTER ONE

From the way the sky looked, the small midwestern town of Meadorville was in for a real storm. The dark, bilious clouds marched angrily across the threatening horizon as Taryn Oliver peered anxiously out the window of her grandfather's parlor. Because of the high heat and humidity the town had experienced all day, Taryn viewed the approaching storm with mixed emotions.

"It looks like it's going to storm, Grandpa," Taryn remarked, a worried frown on her pensive features, as she brushed her red hair away from her face.

The distinguished, elderly white-haired man who had just walked into the room, chuckled softly as he walked over and switched on the lamp next to the comfortable blue and white wing chair Taryn was standing by. "Let 'er rain," he consented merrily. "No one can deny that we need the moisture."

"Yes, I suppose that's true," she mused, "but I certainly hope it isn't going to be a bad storm."

Martin Lassiter smiled, then patted his grand-daughter on the arm affectionately. "No need for you

9

to worry. It's just another one of those late summer thunderstorms that come through here periodically. Nothing unusual about that."

Taryn let the curtain drop back in place, his words of comfort doing little to still her mounting apprehension. "I know, Grandpa, but I've always hated—" She paused and listened intently for a moment to the muted sound of a siren in the distance. "Is that what I think it is?"

Martin cocked an ear, a frown crossing his pleasant features. "Sounds like the civil defense sirens."

"Civil defense . . . Oh, goodness, maybe we'd better turn the radio on." Taryn's face had gone pale as she brushed past her grandfather and quickly hurried toward the kitchen. Unless there had been a malfunction, there would be no reason for the sirens to be activated except in case of enemy attack or—a tornado warning! Either thought made her grow weak with fear as she switched on the radio sitting on the kitchen cabinet.

The voice of the local DJ issuing curt, concise instructions filled the room ". . . residents are advised to seek shelter immediately. We repeat. There has been a funnel spotted on the ground twenty miles from Meadorville, moving in a northeasterly direction at approximately thirty miles per hour. All residents are advised to take shelter immediately. . . ."

"Oh, Grandpa." Taryn's face paled as she reached out to grip his hand in fear. "What do we do now?"

"Don't get upset. Just because it's twenty miles

away doesn't necessarily mean it will strike Meadorville," he said calmly. "But we will go down to the basement."

"Basement?" Taryn's mind refused to function properly for a moment. She had been away for over a year and had completely forgotten that there *was* a basement under the large two-story home.

"Taryn." Martin patted her reassuringly on the shoulder as he walked past her, heading for the front door. "Pull yourself together, dear. I'm going to open the front door so that the neighbors can get in. There are several families in the area who don't have a basement, and I'm sure they'll all want to take shelter here. You go on down and start gathering up the candles and the battery-powered radio I keep down there in a box marked 'Emergency.' There should be a couple of flashlights on the shelf beside the box, too."

Taryn's legs felt like rubber as she followed her grandfather through the house listening to the sound of the rising wind. She glanced uneasily out the window and saw the tops of the huge old oaks surrounding the house sway restlessly as the sky turned the bright day into premature darkness.

The sound of loud, insistent pounding filled the house as Martin hurried toward the front door and pulled it open. A small group of frightened people surged inside, babbling nervously about the approaching storm, trying to reassure each other that it

11

would surely miss the town, as it had done so many times in the past.

"I hope you don't mind, Martin," a large heavyset man apologized as he rushed by Taryn carrying a sleeping child in his arms.

"Of course not, Ferris. You know you're always welcome to share my home in times like these," Martin told him. "Everyone just follow Taryn. She was on her way down to set out the supplies."

Taryn suddenly snapped out of her stupor and once more became her usual efficient self. She hurriedly led the group to the basement stairs and within minutes had them comfortably settled, with candles, a radio, and flashlights readily at hand.

Assuring them that she would be back shortly, she raced back up the stairs to see if she could be of assistance to others coming in out of the storm.

An indeterminate number of people were swarming in the front door as she anxiously made her way over to her grandfather. Her greatest fear at the moment was that the storm would hit before Martin would take shelter. Her grandfather's life had been devoted to seeing to other people's needs before his, and she knew today would be no different.

"Come on, Grandpa," she urged, taking his arm and steering him toward the stairway. "Just leave the front door open for any latecomers."

"I will . . . I will. I just want to check on . . . things," he said quietly.

"I'm sure things . . . are fine, Grandpa," she assured him quickly. "No one's going anywhere."

"I know, but I still want to check," he replied stubbornly. "You go on down to the basement and I'll be along in a few minutes."

"Do you promise? The storm sounds like it's getting closer," Taryn pointed out in a voice filled with anxiety.

"I promise. Now run along, worrywart," he chuckled as he disappeared through a set of double wooden doors on his left.

Taryn shook her head. That Grandpa! Always the businessman first!

The front door burst open again as a loud clap of thunder was followed by a jagged streak of lightning that illuminated the room. A man was struggling through the door, his arms full of potted plants, African violets, and a large birdcage. Inside the cage a bright green parrot was talking in a high, shrill pitch, nervously swinging back and forth on its perch. Following the man was a rotund older woman, holding a cat, a goldfish, and a photograph album. She had three dogs on leashes trailing behind her.

"Oh, good afternoon, dearie. Is Martin in?" the woman inquired.

"He's in the other room right now. Did you want to use the basement?" Taryn stepped forward to relieve the woman of some of her pets, her eyes discreetly watching the man standing inside the door. His rich, wavy brown hair was plastered to his head

13

from the downpour that had opened up only minutes before. Although Taryn had been raised in this small midwestern town, the woman and her male companion were unfamiliar to her.

"You must be Taryn." The woman stepped forward and smiled. "Martin's told me a lot about you! I moved here a little over six months ago, and I've gotten to know your grandfather quite well," she chattered as they moved hurriedly toward the stairway. As they descended the stairs, it sounded as if the state zoo were moving into the cramped concrete shelter.

"By the way, my name's Sadie Mullins, and I bought the old Hoskins house," the woman called over her shoulder as they threaded their way down the winding steps.

"Nice to meet you," Taryn responded politely as she tried to still the squirming cat she held in her arms. She noticed the man had still not uttered a word.

The sound of the storm was increasing as it eerily rattled the large old house. Taryn turned to peer over her shoulder at the man following her. "Are you Mrs. Mullins's son?"

"No." He reached down and irritably thumped the cage holding the screaming parrot. "Pipe down, will you, fella?"

Taryn swallowed nervously, hoping that Sadie wasn't one of those women caught up in the current craze of marrying younger men. *Much* younger men!

This man didn't look to be over thirty-five. "Are you her husband?"

A distasteful set of the coldest gray eyes that Taryn had ever seen met her hazel ones. "No. I'm not her husband!" he returned coolly.

"Okay. I give up." Taryn smiled guiltily. "Who are you?" If he wasn't going to introduce himself, she would seize the initiative and ask.

"The name's Reed Montgomery. And I'm no kin to Mrs. Mullins whatsoever. I happened to be passing through when the radio began forecasting the approaching storm. I thought I'd be able to make it to a motel for the night before the storm hit, but time ran out. I left my car out on the street and ran for the nearest ditch. I happened to meet Mrs. Mullins running across the yard—or trying to." He held the birdcage out in front of him and shook it soundly. "Unfortunately, I offered to help her with Motormouth and her potted plants. I said knock it off, bird!" He glared at the parrot sternly.

"Do you live around here?" Taryn grimaced as the bird screeched even louder. They had paused on the steps to let Sadie work her considerable bulk, along with her bundles, down the narrow stairway.

"Just passing through," he grunted, unconsciously banging the birdcage loudly against the wall as they began to make their way once again down the tight enclosure.

Taryn heard him mutter a low curse under his breath as his feet slid down two unexpected steps,

15

sending the parrot into another screaming fit and fern petals flying wildly. By the time they'd reached the bottom of the stairs, Reed seemed to have reached the bottom of his patience as well.

"Oh, Malcolm! You're being such a naughty little boy today," Sadie scolded lovingly as she took the cage out of Reed's hand and shook her finger disapprovingly at her little feathered friend. "You're going to make the nice man think you act like this all the time!" She turned to face Reed, her motherly features beaming. "Isn't he a doll!"

Reed's face definitely disputed that statement, but he replied politely. "Yes, ma'am. He's real cute." His gray eyes turned guiltily toward the ceiling.

"Grandpa!" Taryn felt a tremendous relief a few minutes later when she saw Martin Lassiter come down the basement steps. "Is everything all right?"

"I've tried to secure things as much as possible," he said quietly as he reached for one of the flashlights and checked the batteries. "What's the latest news on the storm, Ferris?"

Ferris was glued to a radio, listening attentively to the continuous coverage of the storm. "The twister is still on the path to Meadorville leaving thousands of dollars' worth of destruction in its path. As of yet they haven't given any estimate on death or personal injuries," Ferris reported in a shaky voice.

Two of the small children whimpered in fright as their mother pulled them closer and whispered consolingly to them.

16

"Nothing to worry about," Martin assured everyone in a steady voice. "We're good and safe right where we are."

"Unless the building falls in on us, or the gas pipes blow," Reed muttered tensely under his breath.

"You're a real optimist, aren't you?" Taryn uttered irritably, hoping that no one else had heard his thoughtless remark. Everyone was visibly upset, except her grandfather, who had always had nerves of steel.

"I consider myself more of a realist," he said as he sank down on the floor against the concrete wall of the basement to await the outcome of the storm.

Taryn noticed that his clothes were soaking wet. She searched through a pile of folded linen, withdrawing a large white sheet and handing it to him. "Here, you can dry yourself with this. We don't have any men's clothing—at least not down here," she added.

Reed glanced at her in surprise, then took the proffered gift gratefully. "Thanks." With deft, sure strokes he toweled his thick hair dry and mopped ineffectually at his wet clothing. A few minutes later he withdrew a comb from his back pocket and hurriedly worked the thick waves carefully back into place. Taryn was mesmerized by that dark mass of hair. It was extremely attractive, styled in a cut perfect for his rugged masculine features.

Glancing up unexpectedly, he narrowed his eyes

17

in suspicion as he saw her watching him. "What's wrong?" he confronted her warily.

"Oh . . . nothing." She felt a slow blush staining her cheeks red. How embarrassing that he had caught her staring at him like that!

"Did you say you were just passing through town?" she asked, hoping to divert his attention.

"Yeah, I'm on my way to New Mexico." He placed his comb back in his pocket and looked around him. "Where am I, anyway?"

"You mean, what town are you in?"

"Yeah."

"Meadorville. Population six hundred and forty-two people—No, I take that back. Grandpa said Betsy Merrill had her baby last week, so I guess that makes the population six hundred and forty-three. One of the biggest little towns in the Midwest!" Taryn smiled proudly.

"Never heard of it," he admitted.

"Most people haven't. But it's a lovely town. I've lived here all my life until about a year ago. By the way, my name's Taryn." She sighed and shifted around on the hard concrete floor to get more comfortable. "I've only been back home about a week. I wish now I'd waited another week! Are you a salesman?" The last three sentences had been said all in one breath as Taryn turned to face Reed.

Reed looked at her blankly. "Attorney. A criminal attorney."

"Criminal attorney! How interesting. I once

18

thought about being a lawyer, but that was a long time ago. I'm afraid I've met some pretty shady lawyers in the last few years. Not that they were all crooked—" She broke off, leaving her sentence hanging in midair after she saw the defensive glare Reed was directing at her. "Anyway, I really haven't decided on what I want to do with my life yet. I used to think I knew exactly what I wanted, but that was before I got married. Now I'm having to rethink my whole future. Grandpa wants me to stay here and work with him again, which wouldn't really be all that bad since I was raised in the business and have helped him ever since my parents died. They died when I was sixteen, you know, leaving me with Grandpa. That was over nine years ago—it's hard to believe—well, anyway, after I married I thought I would probably go into the insurance business with my husband and I would have been happy doing that," she assured with an earnest nod of her head. "I would have been happy doing anything Gary wanted; anything but racing those darn motorcycles that he insisted on racing! I always told him he was going to get himself killed." She paused for a moment, thinking about Gary. She was determined not to get choked up about it again. Especially not now—and not around a stranger. She turned her thoughts back to Reed. "But that's all in the past and everyone tells me I'm young and can make a new life—"

"Excuse me," Reed said curtly.

"Yes?" Taryn looked expectantly at him, unaware

that she had been talking so much. Talking had always been one of her downfalls.

"Do you mind? I'd like to hear the radio." He looked at her as if she were going to start frothing at the mouth any minute.

"Oh . . . I've been talking too much, haven't I?"

"Well—" Reed paused and looked uneasy. "I don't mean to be rude, but I've got a lot of things on my mind. I should have been in Santa Fe hours ago, and the way it looks, I'm not going to make it until this time tomorrow."

"Oh? Do you have pressing business to attend to?" She didn't want to sound pushy; still, they were in such close quarters, it seemed unfriendly of her not to inquire about his destination.

"Pressing business?" His grin was mischievous. "I suppose it's 'pressing.' I'm on my way to a wedding."

"Oh, how nice!" she gushed. "Are you the best man—usher—?"

"Groom."

"Oh—" Her smile died a sudden death. "How nice," she repeated in a tone somehow lacking the enthusiasm of moments earlier. Naturally a man as good-looking as Reed would be either married or spoken for. Not that she would be interested, even if he wasn't. She had just come through a traumatic period in her life and certainly wasn't ready for another relationship yet. Gary had only been dead about a year and his ghost was still very much alive in her heart. Nevertheless, it was with extreme difficulty that she turned her eyes away from Reed's obvious masculine attributes, which were noticeable against his wet clothing.

A streak of longing shot through her as she willed her mind away from the mental picture it had suddenly thrust upon her. This was the first time that she had been so blatantly made aware that sexually appealing men still existed in the world. For longer than she cared to admit, her mind and body had been totally numb, simply living from day to day without any thoughts of the past or future. For a brief moment it angered her to think that her body was going to betray her and start feeling again.

"I wonder what's going on." Reed shifted around restlessly, trying to hear the radio Ferris had glued to his ear. "The storm's sure taking its own sweet time getting here."

"I'm sure it would be terribly upset to think you were anxiously awaiting its arrival and it was late," Taryn observed, still irritated by the feelings he had aroused in her. Why did his pants have to fit so tight! He was undoubtedly one of those crooked lawyers she had referred to earlier. In her opinion, *all* crooked lawyers wore their pants too tight.

"All I'm getting is a bunch of static on the radio now," Ferris called from across the room. "Has anyone else brought a radio with them?"

The occupants of the room all shook their heads no as Ferris sighed and went back to fiddling with the tuner.

"I'm getting tired of sitting here." Reed got to his feet, towering over Taryn like a giant. "I'm going upstairs to check things out. It's probably all blown over by now."

"Oh, gosh, do you think you should?" She was instantly on her feet beside him. "I really don't think it's safe yet—"

"Hey, let me worry about that, okay?" He sounded unnecessarily cranky to her. "This waiting around drives me crazy!" He began to pace the floor fretfully.

"I know it's hard, but we're relatively safe here," Taryn argued. "I'm sure you're right and it will miss us, but I still think we should wait for an all-clear signal from the radio. I've lived with these warnings all my life, and we never have had a tornado hit Meadorville," she finished encouragingly.

Reed continued his pacing for another few minutes before he sank resignedly back down on the floor, burying his hands in the thickness of his hair. "What a hell of a mess!"

Taryn smiled to herself. He was beginning to remind her of her late husband. Gary Oliver had had the same streak of impatience. A shaft of pain coursed through her at the thought of her husband. They had been married such a short time. Only six weeks before his death. And they had only dated a few weeks before they married. Her love affair with Gary had been short, painful, but joyously happy.

"Where did you say you lived?" Reed's impatient voice sliced through her thoughts.

"I've been living in Georgia the last year," she answered quietly, trying to overcome the lump that had risen tightly in her throat. The loud crying of one of the children wanting to get off its parent's lap was beginning to grate on her nerves.

They were sitting next to each other again, so it would be close to impossible for Reed to have not noticed the thin film of tears that now misted her eyes.

"Hey," he said softly, reaching over to wipe gently at the wetness slipping down her cheeks, "it's going to be all right. I'm sure the storm will go around. There's nothing to be frightened of. I just get a little antsy when I'm put in a tight spot." His smile was supportive. "I suppose I'm dreading to face Elaine and her mother. Did I mention I was supposed to be in New Mexico tonight by six o'clock?"

Elaine must be the intended bride, Taryn surmised as she hurriedly wiped at her rising tears. "You probably won't be delayed over a few hours. You can call your fiancée from here if you like. I'm sure she'll understand the delay."

"I'm not." He said flatly, "Elaine likes to have things run on schedule."

"When is the wedding?"

"Next Saturday, exactly one week from today, but there's a string of parties we have to attend," he grumbled.

"Well, you might have to miss one or two of the parties, but I'm sure you'll make the wedding."

"Hey"—Reed reached back over and offered her the corner of the large sheet he had used earlier—"everything's going to be okay, I tell you."

"Please forgive me, Mr. Montgomery, but this has nothing to do with the storm," she apologized with a shaky laugh, wiping the corner of her eyes with the huge sheet. "It's just that your impatience reminded me of someone I used to know. . . ."

"From all the waterworks, you must have known him well," Reed observed softly.

"Yes, very well. He was my husband."

"Was?"

"He was killed in a motorcycle accident six weeks after our marriage, didn't I tell you?" The words still brought almost unbelievable pain when they were spoken.

"Yes. It must have been rough for you," Reed murmured uneasily, glancing away.

"Yes, it was," she agreed.

The sudden sound of an explosion filled the small basement as the occupants snapped to attention.

"What was that?" Taryn lurched toward Reed, her body trembling uncontrollably as his two strong arms unexpectedly caught her up against his broad chest.

"If I were a gambling man, I'd say the storm has just arrived," Reed predicted grimly, pulling her closer into the shelter of his arms.

The roar of the wind was deafening as the occupants of the basement cringed in terror, praying the old house would not blow in on them, or any gas line erupt, posing yet another threat to the already growing list. No one spoke above the fury of the storm as they grouped together in a frightened huddle. Except for the handful of small children crying, the room was filled with nothing but the sound of the angry roar of the storm venting its fury on the small town of Meadorville.

CHAPTER TWO

Taryn closed her eyes and buried her face in the comfort of Reed's neck, her arms clasped tightly around him. He smelled so clean—so masculine. The faint aroma of soap and a woodsy aftershave drifted pleasantly up to her. For a second, the feel of a man's body next to hers was a jolt. It had been a long time since she had been held in such strong, capable arms and she had nearly forgotten how comforting it could be. She was instantly ashamed of such intimate thoughts, especially in view of Reed's being another woman's soon-to-be-husband. But as long as he never knew how much she was enjoying the sensation of being in his arms, what harm could there be? Her only concern at the moment was trying to keep his attention diverted from the way her body was automatically responding to being pressed against him. Her breasts unexpectedly felt tight and full, aching for the touch of a man, a man who could ease the longings and sexual frustration that suddenly seemed to be overwhelming her. They both moved closer, their bodies fusing together intimately.

For one crazy instant, Taryn could have sworn he was beginning to respond to *her* soft curves crushed against his rigid thighs.

The storm continued to scream vehemently as Reed and Taryn cowered in each other's tight embrace.

After what seemed an eternity to the occupants of the basement, the wind began to die down and heavy rain began to fall from the angry heavens.

Raising her head, Taryn encountered the cool gray of Reed's eyes looking at her in an oddly disturbing manner. They were still locked tightly in each other's arms, a position Taryn was reluctant to give up.

"Are you all right?" he asked in a voice that wasn't quite steady.

"I think so. Are you?"

He gave a shaky laugh. "I'm not sure."

They both stepped out of their embrace, embarrassedly avoiding each other's gaze.

"Anyone hurt?" Reed called out worriedly.

"No one's hurt, thank God," Ferris called back, gathering a crying child back into his arms. "What about you?"

"We're fine." He looked dazedly around, still trying to pull his senses together.

"Grandpa?" Taryn moved across the room, searching for her grandfather's familiar face. The group of friends and neighbors were beginning to mill around, relief evident in their voices as they relived the past few minutes. "Has anyone seen Grandpa?"

she asked again, pushing her way through the maze of bodies.

"He was here just before the storm hit," Ferris supplied helpfully as he sat the child back down on the floor. "Hey, Martin! Where are you hiding?"

There was no answer as all eyes began to search the room for the missing Martin.

"Maybe he's already gone back upstairs." Reed spoke reassuringly from Taryn's side.

"Oh, no—surely he hasn't. There's not been time," Taryn said in disbelief.

"I'll run up and check," Reed offered, moving swiftly to the bottom of the staircase.

"I'm going with you." Taryn hurried to his side, forgetting for the moment the dangers that could still exist.

"No. You stay here," Reed ordered curtly as he bounded up the stairs. "I'll be right back."

As he reached the top of the stairway, the sound of heavy rain pounding on the roof met his ears. His eyes quickly assessed the destruction of the room, noting with relief that the house seemed to have been spared the brunt of the storm. It was pitch-dark now as he picked his way through, shining his flashlight over the various pieces of debris scattered throughout the house. Broken glass from blown-out windows littered the floors, slowing down his progress considerably. Reed hadn't noticed how large the old house was when he had hastily entered it an hour ago, but he noticed now that it was indeed huge. A comfortable two-story interior met his dim vision as he moved about, barely able to ascertain the function of each room he passed through. In the front part of the house there was what seemed to be a large parlor, furnished tastefully in French Provincial furniture. What appeared to be an office sat directly across from the parlor. Two large wooden doors were closed and locked immediately to the right of the office, and farther on down the hall were an additional two rooms with their doors closed. Reed couldn't help but wonder what an elderly man and his granddaughter would need with all this space!

Stumbling over a limb that had been blown through the front window, Reed reached out to steady himself on the door handle of a closed room. The door swung open, throwing Reed into the dark interior. He swore silently as he heard the flashlight he had brought up from the basement hit the floor and roll away. Dropping to his knees, he began to feel his way across the floor, looking for it. When the flashlight hit the floor, its beam had gone out, making it virtually impossible for Reed to try to regain his only source of light. Deciding he would have to go back down to the basement for another flashlight, he rose and started blindly to feel his way across the room. Just as he thought he had made it, his foot encountered a solid object lying on the floor close to a window that had been blown out. Kneeling down, he ran his hands over the object in puzzlement. Instantly he jerked back, his heart racing frantically.

Deciding that he surely hadn't felt what he thought he had, he returned his hands to examine the still form once more. This time the fine hair at the base of his neck stood erect. Jerking his hand back once more, he rose swiftly to his feet. Whatever was lying on the floor was cold, and very, very still.

Could Taryn's grandfather have wandered in here and fallen? Reed earnestly hoped not. It seemed to him that the slight, trembling woman he had held in his arms earlier had already been through quite enough in the last year without suffering the additional loss of her grandfather.

If he only had a flashlight! He stood up and stifled a sneeze. Darn! His allergy was acting up. He frowned. That was strange. The only thing he was allergic to was flowers. Edging slowly around the fallen object, he hurriedly made his way back out of the room, fumbling back down the path he had come, trying to shake off the sense of eeriness that assailed him. This whole thing was beginning to give him the creeps! He had never been one to crawl around in dark places. Even as a small boy, he had never indulged in haunted houses, visiting graveyards at the mysterious witching hour of midnight, or in any other strange ideas his friends were always coming up with. Strong, powerful Reed Montgomery had barely acknowledged Halloween, let alone gone running around after things that go bump in the dark! Give him the strong light of day anytime! Not that he was particularly afraid of anything; he considered himself as brave as the next guy, but he preferred to look the enemy straight in the eye, and know exactly what he was up against.

Cautiously rounding the last corner, he let out a yelp of pure terror as a cold hand reached out and rigidly clamped down on his wrist.

"Did you find him?" A female voice drifted impatiently out of the pit of blackness.

Issuing an expletive, Reed sagged weakly against the wall, his heart hammering wildly in his chest.

"Did I frighten you?" Taryn apologized as she stepped over and tried to help support his sagging frame.

"What do you mean by sneaking up on me that way!" he yelled.

Taryn's hand dropped from his shoulder. If he was going to take that attitude, he could stand on his own!

"You don't have to get so testy, Mr. Montgomery," she said in a defensive voice. "I wasn't sneaking up on you!"

"Next time, let someone know when you come slinking up like that," he snapped as he shoved his shirttail back down in his trousers. "You walk like a cat!"

"I'm very sorry! In our business we have been taught to walk and *speak* quietly. Something you've obviously never been taught—"

"Have you got an extra flashlight with you?" he interrupted, making it abundantly clear that he

31

wasn't interested in what she had, or had not, been taught.

"Not an extra one, but I do have mine—"

"Good." He snatched it out of her hand before she could protest. "Stay here."

"I will not! Not in the dark! I'm coming with you." She grabbed hold of his belt and he dragged her along behind him.

"Can't you walk?" he fussed as they picked their way back through the rubble.

"I'm walking. Just slow down! Oh, dear, has the storm destroyed the house completely?" she fretted as they made their way slowly toward the front of the house.

"No, actually I think there will be very little damage when the rubble is cleared away. There're several windows blown out, but that can be easily taken care of." He shook the dimming flashlight irritably, trying to get it to come back on. Finally a faint, weak ray shot out of the cylinder. "These batteries are almost gone."

"I know. Grandpa forgot to rotate them."

"Great! Simply great!" He pointed the weak light toward the center of the room, trying to make out the shape of objects. "Why don't you step outside and take a look around? Maybe your grandfather's decided to do the same thing." He wanted to get her out of the way so he could take a closer look at what he had discovered earlier. "Just be careful. There may be some power lines down," he warned.

"Okay, but I'll need the flashlight," she agreed hesitantly.

"Are there any matches or candles up here?"

"Yes, I think so. Why?"

"Get them for me. I'll need a light to check around. I think it's safe to strike a match. If there were any gas leaks we would have smelled them by now." Taryn took the flashlight he offered. "Meet me back here in a few minutes," he ordered curtly.

The rain was still coming down in sheets as Taryn made her way into the kitchen. She was sure that her grandfather wouldn't have gone out in this kind of downpour, but she had the feeling Reed was in no mood to argue, so she hurried to find the matches and candles.

A low moan met her ears as she searched hurriedly through the bottom cabinet drawer. Feeling her way over to the sound, she turned the weak light back on and gasped when she saw her grandfather's crumpled form lying on the floor.

"Reed!" she shouted, kneeling down next to the still figure and feeling for a pulse. Thankfully, she found a strong steady beat and she breathed a sigh of relief.

"What?" Reed shouted. She could hear him bumping into furniture as he tried to fight his way into the kitchen.

"Come in here. I've found Grandpa!"

Reed hurriedly found his way across the dark room and knelt down beside her. "Is he all right?"

33

"I think so. He must have fallen and knocked himself out. Here, hold the light while I get a wet cloth." Within minutes she was back, placing a cold compress to her grandfather's forehead.

Martin moaned softly as Taryn leaned over and spoke loudly to him. "Grandpa, can you hear me?"

Another low groan escaped his lips as he reached out and grasped her hand. "I think I've broken my leg."

"Just lie still. We'll get you some help," she consoled, patting his hand gently. She turned to Reed and whispered urgently, "We've got to get an ambulance."

"That's probably close to impossible," he returned quickly. "If there've been many injuries—"

Taryn slapped her head in exasperation. "What am I talking about! There isn't an ambulance service here."

Reed looked at her anxiously. "Now what?"

"I don't know . . . let me think. Foster! Foster Savage and his wife help Grandpa in the business." She bit her lip thoughtfully. "I haven't seen Foster tonight, have you?"

Reed looked at her blankly. "Hell, I wouldn't know Foster if he walked up and spit on me!"

"Go look in the cottage in back of the house. And hurry!" she pleaded as she went to run cold water over the cloth again.

Reed ran out the back door and returned in five minutes, fighting for every breath. "There's no one out there," he wheezed. "I nearly tore the door down and there was no answer." He sagged weakly against the kitchen counter.

"Oh, I just remembered. He was taking his wife to the doctor this afternoon. They must have gotten caught in the storm somewhere. Go down and get Ferris. Tell him to bring one of the cots from downstairs. We'll have to get Grandpa to the clinic by ourselves."

"The house . . . is it gone?" Martin tried to rise from the floor.

"No, just lie back, Grandpa. The house has very little damage to it." Taryn pushed the jacket she had just removed from him under his head for a pillow.

"Martha. Did you check on Martha?"

"Not yet, but I will. You don't need to worry about a thing, Grandpa," she repeated, looking around anxiously for Reed's return. In a few minutes he came bounding back into the room, dragging Ferris and a large cot with him. He was still fighting to draw a normal breath as he helped lift Martin gently up on the cot. "Listen," he gasped between gulps of fresh air, "I think there's someone else hurt up there in that room on the left side of the office."

Taryn paused in draping a light blanket over Martin and thought about the room he was describing. She glanced up sheepishly at Reed and asked, "What do you mean 'hurt'?"

"I mean, while I was up there looking for your grandfather I stumbled over someone lying on the

35

floor. At first I thought it was your grandfather, but apparently it wasn't. Since it was so dark, I don't know if it's a man or woman, but I *am* sure it was a body!"

"Oh, dear. That was probably Martha," Taryn mused worriedly.

"Well, the poor woman needs help! We'd better try to get both of them to the doctor at the same time," he urged adamantly. "She's out cold!"

"Just calm down," Taryn said quietly as she leaned over and kissed her grandfather on the cheek. "Ferris will take you out to the car—"

"No . . . the car has a flat tire. Foster was going to buy a new spare on his way home this afternoon," Martin said weakly.

"Oh." Taryn thought for a moment. "Then I suppose we'll have to use the business car."

"That seems to be our only alternative," Martin agreed.

"Okay, Ferris, you go ahead and get Grandpa loaded in the limousine and Reed and I will take care of Martha." She looked at Reed hopefully. "Or would you rather load Grandpa and let Ferris help me with Mrs. Feagan?"

"Let Ferris load Martin and I'll help you."

"Good!" Ferris heaved a tremendous sigh of relief. "I'd rather see to Martin than have to help with Martha." He hurriedly pushed the stretcher out the back door.

36

Reed gave Taryn a cocky grin. "What's the matter with Ferris. Don't he and Martha get along?"

"Why, of course he got along with Martha. She's taught school in Meadorville for over fifty years," Taryn scolded. "Everyone loved her."

Reed shrugged his broad shoulders. "Just wondering. He acted mighty relieved that he wasn't going to have to help you with her. I'll go get the other cot."

"I don't think we'll need it," she said evasively as they made their way back through the dark house.

"Yes, we will," he stubbornly persisted. "I'm telling you, the woman's hurt!"

"Trust me. We'll take care of things without a cot," Taryn soothed as she opened the door on the left side of the office. "Here, light this candle and set it on the table in back of you." She handed him a candle and a box of matches.

"She's still out, huh? I told you she was in bad shape." The candle flared into light, casting a weak, wavering shadow across the room. Reed paused and sniffed the air suspiciously. "What's that sickly sweet smell? Smells like flowers." At the mere mention of the word he sneezed explosively.

"Gesundheit!"

"Thanks. What do you want me to do?"

"I think we'll just pick her up and lay her on the sofa until I can get . . . things arranged again."

Reed walked over to kneel down beside Taryn. He looked at the woman's face he had touched earlier.

"Gosh, she's pretty old," he said sympathetically. "I hope she hasn't broken anything."

"Yes." Taryn touched the weathered face tenderly. "She is old. For as long as I can remember, Martha Feagan has been such a vital part of Meadorville." Taryn turned to face Reed. "I'll bet she's responsible for over three fourths of the population's education in this town. I wish you could have known her. Here, help me lift her onto the sofa."

The blood vessels in Reed's neck nearly exploded as he grunted strenuously, trying to heave the dead weight onto the couch. "Ho . . . holy cow," he groaned, "Martha is going to have to cut down on the late-night pizzas and seconds on potatoes!"

It was all Taryn could do to lift her end, too, but they both managed, and in seconds they had Martha Feagan resting comfortably. Reed stood staring down at the quiet figure in repose. "Do you think she'll be all right? I suppose the storm made her faint." He clucked his tongue in sympathy. "Poor old thing looks white as a sheet." He sneezed loudly once more.

"Gesundheit!" Taryn repeated.

"Darn it!" he groaned, reaching into his back pocket and dragging out a large white handkerchief. "Are there any flowers around here?"

"Are you serious? There's a whole roomful," Taryn said, confirming his worst fear. "I told you Martha was well loved by this town. Can you come over here for a minute? I want to set the casket back upon the

38

pedestal, then I'll gather up the—Reed?" She turned to check on him, wondering why the room had grown so silent.

Reed had turned back around to look at Taryn, *his* face ghostly white now. "Set the what, where?" he asked.

"I said, can you give me a hand with the casket? This one is very heavy. It must have been one heck of a wind that went through this room. I don't think I can manage it by myself," she mused thoughtfully.

"Cask-et?" he repeated in a hoarse whisper.

Taryn smiled tolerantly. Here we go again! He was going to have the typical reaction all strangers had when she told him what he had accidentally stumbled into while seeking shelter from the storm. "Now, there's nothing to be alarmed about, Reed, all you have to do is help—Reed!" She rushed forward and tried to break his fall, but they both went down, his large frame wilting heavily on top of hers. Powerful, strong Reed Montgomery had fainted clean as a whistle!

Taryn was sure he had broken her arm as she tried to crawl out from beneath him, every bone in her body aching. For the life of her she didn't know why everyone always got so upset about being in a funeral home!

Giving one authoritative shove, she pushed his limp body off her and struggled to her feet. "Reed? Reed!" She gave his face a sharp slap, trying to get a response out of him. "Wake up!"

Reed's six feet plus lay stretched serenely out on the floor, an angelic smile plastered to his face. No amount of pleading brought him back to the present.

With a sigh of disgust she picked up a vase and removed the flowers, then stood back as she dashed the cold water on his face.

With a loud, unpleasant oath he sat straight up and looked around him in bewilderment. His eyes focused on Martha Feagan lying quietly on the sofa.

"Oh, good Lord," he groaned, burying his face in his hands and lying back down. "Tell me it's a bad dream," he pleaded in a muffled voice.

"You are acting very childish," Taryn said sternly, walking around the room to straighten up the damage the storm had done. "I'm not saying you're the first one to act this way, but I certainly think you're old enough to be a little braver about the situation."

Another sneeze ripped forcefully through him. "Get those flowers out from under my nose!" He irritably shoved a bouquet of carnations away from him. "My allergy is killing me. . . ." His eyes flickered toward Martha. "Let me rephrase that . . . my allergy's acting up," he corrected quickly.

"I'm sorry, there's nothing I can do about that. You'll have to simply stay out of this room if you're allergic to flowers."

"That you can count on," he moaned. "I want out of here."

"You're free to go any time you choose . . ." she

40

said, patiently rearranging a bouquet of gladiolus and mums.

He was on his feet streaking by her like a bolt of lightning when he felt a firm hand clamp down on the back of his shirt collar. ". . . just as soon as you help me get Martha's casket set back on the pedestal and Grandpa to the hospital," she finished sternly.

"Oh, come on! Give me a break, Taryn!"

"It is not going to hurt you to lend me a hand. After all, this is an emergency," she told him curtly, "and supposedly you're a big boy now and know that the boogie man isn't going to jump out and get you."

"The 'boogie man' wasn't exactly what I had in mind," he grumbled as he backed farther away from the sofa.

"Rubbish! Pure rubbish. Being in the funeral business is one of the most gratifying experiences a person could ever wish to have. Think about it, Reed. I'm privileged to do some of the last things done on this earth for people who have been a part of my life ever since I came into the world. You should have no fear of the dead. Why, if you had been here three days ago, I would have shown you Lila Stewart, a lovely old saint who was my Sunday school teacher all during my teen-age years. They're the same people they always were, Reed. They're moms and dads, grandparents, aunts, uncles, children . . . all of them were loved and cherished," she finished softly.

"Fine! If you like your job, then more power to you, but as far as I'm concerned"—he glanced over at the sofa and shuddered—"this place gives me the willies and I'm cutting out just as soon as I get your grandfather loaded in the car and that"—he shuddered again—"box set back up on the pedestal."

"That's perfectly all right with me," she returned calmly. She could sympathize with his fear, but she honestly didn't understand it.

"You can just get your nose out of the air, lady," he said curtly. "You're talking to a guy who'll drive five miles out of his way to keep from passing a cemetery!"

Ten minutes later they stepped out of the room and securely closed the door. "Now, that wasn't so bad, was it?" Taryn chided as they walked back toward the kitchen.

Reed grimaced and made a face. He had thought he was going to throw up when she made him help her lift Martha back in the . . . The very thought of the casket made him shudder for the fifth time in the last ten minutes.

"Are you cold?"

"No. Let's just get your grandfather to the hospital and then I'm leaving."

"But it's so late!" Taryn protested. "And all the roads will probably be closed due to the storm. You better plan on staying here tonight—"

"Forget it!" he stated bluntly. "If I have to crawl on my hands and knees out of this town, I'm not staying in your *house* tonight!"

"Baby!"

"Ghoul!"

"There's no need for sarcasm," she pointed out resentfully.

"Then get off my back. I'm not staying here all night and that's final!"

They were still grumbling at each other as they walked out the back door. Reed stopped and looked at the car parked in the driveway. "I suppose the 'business car' you were referring to is that hearse!"

"That's right. Now what's wrong?"

"I'll tell you what's wrong! I'm not going to drive that . . . that thing, that's what's wrong!"

"Oh, for heaven's sake. Why not? It's just a car!"

"I said"—he took a deep breath and gritted his teeth stubbornly—"I am *not* going to drive that hearse. You get such a kick out of your job, *you* drive it!"

"I can't," she admitted guiltily.

"Why not?"

"Because I'm a lousy driver and Grandpa told me never to drive the hearse again under any circumstances. Last time I didn't get the door in the back closed properly and when I swung around the corner too fast, it flew open . . ." Her voice trailed off sheepishly.

Reed's face turned a sickly green. "Oh, hell . . . you mean—"

"Oh, no! Not that! Nothing happened, actually, but

it made Grandpa and the minister so nervous that Grandpa forbade me to drive it again."

"Well, if this isn't a fine kettle of fish!" he muttered angrily, his eyes once more going to the long black limousine sitting in the drive. He nervously chewed on his bottom lip. "What about Ferris? Let him drive it. I owe the rat fink one for what he pulled on me earlier! No wonder he was grinning from ear to ear when I offered to help you with Martha!"

"There's no need to bother Ferris again! Besides, his driving is supposed to be very limited."

"I don't believe you," he said brusquely.

"Well, it's the truth! Ferris likes to tip the bottle some and last time he was caught, Pryor, that's our town sheriff, well, he took his license away from him for a few days, and when he returned it he told him he couldn't drive unless he had to help Grandpa take someone to the cemetery! If you don't believe me, go ask Pryor."

"Go ask Pryor, go ask Pryor," he mimicked childishly. "He was probably as juiced up as old Ferris was!"

"He was not!" she returned indignantly. "He doesn't smoke, cuss, chew tobacco, or run around with other women. He's a decent, law-abiding citizen of Meadorville and I won't hear of you bad-mouthing Pryor!"

"All right." Reed held up his hands in surrender. "I take it back. Ol' Pryor isn't a boozer."

"That's better," Taryn replied in a miffed tone.

44

"He's an idiot."

Taryn glared at him.

"Look, if I'm going to be forced into driving that . . . thing, I want to get it over with. Let's cut the small talk and get on the road."

"That sounds perfectly wonderful to me. I can hardly wait to see your backside fading into the sunset," Taryn said regally as she brushed past him and walked to the back of the hearse. "I prefer to ride with my grandfather."

"And I prefer not to go at all!"

Taryn climbed into the back of the hearse and loudly slammed the door. "Oh, sorry, little baby. I bet you're afraid I'll 'wake the dead,' " she chided as she slid the back glass panel and leaned over his shoulder to taunt him.

"Just stop with the sick jokes!" He started the engine and glanced around him in resignation. "Just wait until I try to explain this to Elaine and her mother!"

With one final shiver, he put the hearse in gear and screeched out of the funeral home parking lot with a loud squeal of tires.

CHAPTER THREE

The town's only clinic was filled to overflowing as the long black hearse pulled up in front and stopped. It seemed to Taryn that most of Meadorville's six hundred and forty-three people must be there, seeking attention for numerous minor injuries.

She stopped several times to offer words of encouragement to a number of people as they brought Martin into the small emergency area that was already overflowing with other cots and stretchers.

Hours later they were still waiting for word on his condition. Taryn leaned tiredly against the wall, trying to mentally block out a child's screams. Reed walked up and handed her a cup of black coffee and suggested they step outside to catch a breath of fresh air.

"I gather you don't like hospitals any more than you do funeral homes," she teased lightly as they sat down on a low brick wall just outside the emergency room.

"You're right. I'm not particularly fond of either one." He took a sip of his coffee and lit a cigarette.

Glancing over in her direction, he belatedly offered the pack to her.

"No, thanks. I don't smoke, and you shouldn't either. They're bad for you," she said, giving him a disapproving frown.

"Is that the truth? I hadn't heard that," he mocked dryly. "Next thing you know, they'll be trying to take artificial sweeteners away from us."

Leaning back against the wall, he took a long drag off his cigarette, then looked up at the clear, starlit sky. "You'd never know there had been a storm earlier this evening, would you?"

"No, it is hard to believe. It sure is a beautiful night now." The low chirping of the tree frogs filled the peaceful night as they sat drinking their coffee and relaxing.

"Did you ever make your call to Elaine?"

Reed took another drag, then flipped his cigarette over the wall. "Yeah. I called her while you were in talking to the doctor."

"The clinic's phones are still working?"

"Yeah, there was a lot of static, but the call went through."

"Good. I hope she understood."

Taryn heard what sounded like a discouraging word come from where Reed was sitting, but he didn't answer her directly.

"It's none of my business, but I think she certainly should understand," Taryn commented. "After all, how could you know that you would be driving

47

through a town and be caught right in the middle of a tornado! That could have happened to Elaine just as easily as it could have happened to you and if she can't see something that simple, then I really don't know what kind of a woman she is," she pointed out quietly. "Probably she's very similar to a friend I once knew. She always wanted things to go her way and when they didn't, she was always looking for an excuse to start an argument, which used to drive me batty because I'm the type of person who would much rather have things go along smoothly than always be in a fight with someone. Wouldn't you? Now, I know that men are different from women, Gary used to always—"

"Excuse me—" he tried to interrupt.

"—laugh and say that of course men were different from women, that's what made it so nice, but I meant that men were different in the sense that they are able to take things in stride a lot easier than women. My grandpa always said that being a woman is like waking up in a whole new world every day, but I don't agree with him. Some people would call him a male chauvinist, but that's not true either. He was raised in a different generation than we were and they viewed a woman's place as being in the home and raising children, which really isn't all that bad. What do you think?"

"Well, I—" he began.

"Personally, I think it would be nice to be able to stay at home and raise my children. Naturally my

48

husband would have to make enough money so that we could all live comfortably on his salary because with the price of groceries alone nowadays—well, it's simply astronomical what it takes to keep a household running! Why, take the price of a roast. Do you have any idea how much an average-size lean rump roast costs today?"

"No, I—"

"Over three dollars a pound, that's what! Unless you're lucky enough to catch it on sale, but that's a horse of a different color. Most of the sales are not really sales. And what about a head of lettuce? You would think you were going to line your shelves with it instead of eat it! Now of course I realize that a lot of women want and need a career and that's all well and good. I don't have any qualms about that, but for me, I think I would—"

"Hey!" Reed let out a loud shrill whistle between his teeth.

Taryn paused, and looked at him in surprise. "Yes?"

"What in the hell are you talking about?"

A rush of color flooded her cheeks. "Oh, dear, have I been rattling on again?"

"Carrying on a conversation with you is like trying to have a discussion with a dot matrix printer," he said tactlessly.

Now that hurt! "Well, excuse me. I was only trying to be friendly," she said in a tone that left him no doubt that she was more than a little put out.

"Do you jabber like this all the time?"

She turned her head away from him haughtily. "If I have something to jabber about. You should try it sometime, Mr. Montgomery. You're entirely too quiet. That makes people automatically suspicious of you."

"A man would have to have nerves of iron to live with you," he grunted, turning back to his coffee.

"My husband never complained," she stubbornly pointed out.

Reed's eyes came back to meet hers. "What was he like?"

Taryn's heart skipped a beat. She wasn't at all sure she wanted to discuss Gary with this arrogant stranger. "He was everything a woman could ever want in a man," she replied factually.

"Everything?" His tone was skeptical.

"Everything. And don't try to dispute that. You didn't know him," she pointed out.

"No, I didn't know him, but I can't help wondering if your opinion of him has been colored somewhat by his death. No one's perfect, Ms. Oliver."

"How dare you!" Taryn's eyes bore heatedly into the gray coldness of his. "Our love was perfect! How can you even suggest that what Gary and I had wasn't wonderful."

"If you'll recall, I didn't say a thing about 'what you and Gary had.' I simply suggested that he may not have been 'everything' a woman could desire."

"He was everything I ever wanted," she said stubbornly.

"Then I'm glad to hear it. You two must have been some of the lucky ones," he returned dryly.

"You're getting married in a week, surely you and Elaine are eager for your wedding day to arrive."

Reed gave a dry laugh. "Eager. Hardly. At least I wouldn't describe myself as eager."

Taryn's mouth dropped open. "You're not looking forward to your own wedding?"

Reed indifferently shrugged his broad shoulders.

"Are you in love with Elaine?"

Again the shoulders lifted and fell disinterestedly.

"Well, this is about the craziest thing I've ever heard of! Why would anyone want to get married if they weren't at all sure they were in love with the person? Why, Gary and I knew without a doubt that we were hopelessly in love with each other a week after we met—"

"Hey!" he cut in impatiently. "You're doing it again."

"Doing what?" she snapped.

"Talking a mile a minute!"

They sat for a while in strained silence before Reed finally picked up the conversation again. "I didn't mean that I didn't like Elaine. I probably like her as much as I'll like any woman, but I'm not marrying her for the supreme reason of being head over heels in love with her."

"That makes no sense whatsoever!" Taryn said

51

tersely. The idea of marriage without overwhelming love for each other was completely foreign to her.

"This may sound cold and calculating to you, but Elaine's and my marriage is in a sense a sound business investment." He shifted around uneasily and reached in his pocket for another cigarette.

"I'm afraid I don't understand," she said. "Are you going to smoke another one of those lung abusers?"

"Well, I sure don't plan on eating it!" He lit another cigarette, defying her scowl.

It was several minutes before he resumed the conversation. "I've known Elaine for several years. We dated off and on all during the time I was going through law school. I got a late start on my profession since my dad died while I was still in high school. I had to support the family until my last sister was through school." He looked at her sharply. "Just so you don't get any wrong idea, I didn't resent that fact in any way."

"I didn't say you did."

"Anyway, Elaine and I have dated for the last four years. Her father has a very lucrative law business in New Mexico, and he's never made any bones about the fact that he would like to take me in as a partner, and Elaine had never made any bones about the fact that she wanted to get married."

"This is getting disgusting," Taryn said crisply. "Are you saying you're going to marry Elaine just so you can step into an established law practice?"

"Something like that," he agreed calmly.

"That stinks."

Reed gave her a solemn look. "Why?"

"Why?" Taryn couldn't believe his gall. "Because it isn't fair to Elaine *or* you," she pointed out.

"What's not fair? I told you, I like Elaine as much as I've ever liked any woman, and since the business is sitting there waiting for me, why not take advantage of it?" He really couldn't see what the problem was.

"Listen to what you're saying, Reed! You *like* Elaine."

"That's right. I like her!"

"You should *love* Elaine!"

"Love." He dismissed the thought with a wave of his hand. "That comes along so very few times in life it isn't even worth discussing. Elaine and I can have a good marriage without . . . all that . . . mush."

"You are unreal." Taryn shook her head in disbelief. "I would hate to think I had to spend my life never knowing the joy of loving someone with all my body, heart, and soul."

"Well, now, apparently that hasn't been your problem, has it? You and your husband were madly in love, to hear you tell it," he said.

"You bet we were!" she stated flatly. "And you are going to be one miserable man if you go through with this farcical marriage."

"Please spare me the sermon. I'm thirty-four years old and should be able to know what I want to do with my life," he replied curtly.

"Yes, you *should*," she agreed tightly.

He threw his cigarette away and chuckled mirth-lessly. "You want to know what I really wanted to do with my life?"

"I assumed you wanted to be a criminal lawyer."

"No, not really. That's what Mom and Dad always wanted me to be. No"—he leaned back against the wall and gazed up into the starry sky, his voice taking on a dreamlike quality—"I also wanted to own a chicken ranch."

"A what?"

"A chicken ranch." He looked at her. "Do you like chickens?"

"I like eggs. I love fried chicken, and chicken and dumplings and chicken pot pie—"

"But do you like chickens themselves?" He sat up straighter and stared at her earnestly.

"I guess so . . . I'd never really thought about it."

"I love them. When I was a kid, I used to get to take care of the animals we had on the farm. That was the good life. No worries other than running the farm every day and taking care of my own family."

"Why don't you buy a chicken farm?" she said crossly. "With all the money you'll be making from your 'business arrangement,' you'll have enough to buy enough chickens to be another Colonel Sanders of New Mexico!"

"You think I'd let people eat my chickens!" he gasped in disbelief.

"Sorry," she grumbled, surprised at how upset he was over the mere thought of anyone touching one

54

feather on his precious chickens! "You wouldn't have to sell the chickens."

"I *have* thought seriously about buying a chicken ranch," he confessed, "but Elaine . . . doesn't like chickens." He sounded like a disappointed child.

"That's what can happen when you marry someone for business reasons, instead of love," she said seriously.

"I suppose you want me to hold out until I find someone who loves chicken ranches?" Their gazes met in the moon-drenched evening. "That may take a lifetime."

"Is that so crazy? I'm sure there're a lot of women out there who would be more than happy to live anywhere you wanted."

"You don't say." He reached over and lightly touched her bottom lip with his finger. "Would you be willing to live on a chicken ranch?"

Taryn's insides quivered at the light, playful touch of Reed's finger. "I would live anywhere with the man I loved."

"Gary was lucky." His finger slipped down to gently caress her creamy complexion. "Have you started dating again?"

"No." Her voice came out small and wistful.

"Why?"

"I'm . . . not ready."

"Still grieving? How long has it been. A year?"

"I'll never forget him."

Reed shook his head thoughtfully. "Hard act for

any man to follow. Don't you miss the companionship a man and woman can have with one another?" His tone was low and suggestive, leaving no doubt in Taryn's mind about what type of "companionship" he was referring to.

"I haven't yet," she answered honestly.

"The day will come when you will," he predicted, his breath fanning softly against her cheek. "Is the man who takes you to bed going to have to fight the ghost of your husband?"

"No, when that day arrives, he'll be taking just me," she whispered sincerely.

"Whether you realize it or not, you're closer to that day than you think. When I held you in my arms earlier tonight, I could sense your response," he cautioned her huskily.

Her eyes dropped shyly away from his. "I was afraid you would."

"Hey"—he tipped her face back up to meet his—"that's nothing to be ashamed about. We all have our needs."

"I know, but I feel like I'm betraying Gary if I feel those . . . needs."

"I understand that's perfectly natural when someone loses their mate. But you're a young, beautiful woman. You're not going to be able to deny those needs forever, you know."

Her hazel eyes darkened as she felt desire surge through her like a hot electrical current. "You shouldn't even be talking to me like this. You're about to be married," she scolded halfheartedly as she watched his mouth slowly descend.

As his lips gently met hers, she froze for a moment, the shock of touching anyone other than her beloved Gary rendering her immobile.

"Relax," he urged cautiously, experimentally brushing his mouth across hers.

"I . . . don't think we should—"

"I don't think we should either, but I figure we're going to anyway, so let's enjoy it."

His mouth closed over hers, as he stood up and drew her tightly against him. Their lips moved together hesitantly at first, tasting, touching, and acquainting themselves with the feel of each other.

"Okay?" he murmured against the sweetness of her mouth.

"Okay," she returned breathlessly.

Their mouths came back to hungrily recapture each other's as they stood pressed tightly together. This time there was no mistaking his response to her lush, ripe curves molding suggestively to his. Taryn had forgotten how quickly she could be aroused by the touch of a man, but she soon remembered as his hand moved caressingly down her back, sensuously stroking her as his tongue began to claim hers. No one had ever kissed her this way. In her marriage to Gary their kisses had been . . . normal . . . satisfying, to be sure . . . but nothing like the way this man was kissing her.

When they parted, they did so with reluctance, his

gray eyes clouded with desire. "You could be a dangerous lady," he whispered, brushing his lips across hers one final time before he pushed her gently out of his arms.

"Why?" Her breathing was as uneven as his, and she felt a great sense of disappointment when he moved away from her.

"You could put a kink in a man's plans, and that would be suicide," he said curtly.

"You mean you're afraid you'll actually feel something for a woman, other than 'like,'" she chided.

"No, I'm not worried about that. But my future is well established and I'm not going to do anything to endanger it."

Taryn's arms dropped to her sides in disgust. "You are hopeless!"

"Look, I hope you didn't read anything into that kiss. It was a matter of a pretty woman being available at a weak moment," he said tactlessly.

"Oh, the kiss meant nothing to me, Mr. Montgomery. As I said before, no one will take my husband's place," she said blithely, fighting the urge to knock his teeth down his throat.

"Good, because the last woman in the world I would get involved with would be a"—he stepped back even farther from her and shivered outwardly —"mortician."

"And the last place in the world I would want to live is on a stinking old chicken farm," she assured him readily.

He acknowledged her statement with a polite nod of his head. "Just so we keep the record straight."

Taryn turned on her heel and started back into the clinic. "I'm going to see about Grandpa!"

Reed trailed along behind her as they entered the emergency room. The doctor looked up as the door opened, and smiled. "There you are, Taryn."

"Hi, Doc. Is Grandpa ready to go home?"

"That's what I wanted to talk to you about. I think I'm going to keep him here for a couple of weeks. He took a pretty bad fall, and besides the broken leg, he's complaining of a headache. In view of his age, I want to watch him closely."

"Whatever you think, Doc." Taryn peeked worriedly behind the curtains at her grandfather. "He's asleep?"

"Yes, we gave him a sedative earlier. You go on home and get some rest yourself. It's been a long night for everyone."

Taryn smiled tiredly and gratefully accepted his offer. "Thanks, I think I will."

"Was there much damage over at your place?" Doc Beason asked as he draped his arm around her waist and walked to the door with her.

"Not a lot. Some, though. I'll have to get someone over to fix the broken windows as soon as possible. Martha's services were to be tomorrow afternoon, but I can change it until Monday."

"Well, let me know if I can help. Can you run things for a while without Martin?"

"Oh, sure. That's no problem."

"Good girl. There shouldn't be any problem with your grandfather, either. A few days rest and he'll be as good as new."

Taryn and Reed walked back out to the hearse and got in. "I'll take you home, then be on my way," he said, starting the engine.

"I still think you should wait until morning," she said coolly.

"No, I've wasted enough time as it is," he returned firmly as he backed the big black limousine out of the parking space.

Fifteen minutes later they pulled into the back of the funeral home and he reached down and turned off the key. "I'll wait until I see a light go on. You know, make sure you got in all right."

"The power probably hasn't come back on yet," she reminded him as she reached for her door handle. "But I still have the candles."

"You'll be okay in there . . ."

"I'll be fine. Martha will keep me company." She couldn't resist the jibe.

Reed's large frame shuddered visibly again. "I'm glad it's you and not me."

"Will you please stop that shuddering? You're going to give me the willies!" she scolded.

"I can't help it. If I had to be in that house another five minutes, I'd croak."

"Look at it this way," she said, grinning, "you'd be in good hands if you did!"

He paled significantly at the unwelcome thought, and let out another long, exaggerated shudder.

Taryn laughed and shook her head in disbelief. "Well, good night, little baby." She opened the car door and stepped out as he exited on the driver's side. He came around to stand next to her, handing her the keys to the limousine.

"Good night. It's been . . . nice meeting you," he returned politely.

"Yes, same here." She looked away from his silvery gaze with frosty aloofness.

"Well, guess I'll go get my car. I left it out front somewhere."

"It's still there, I imagine," she returned in a bored tone, wishing he would hurry up and leave and get it over with.

"If you're ever in Santa Fe, look me up."

"Sure . . . I'll do that."

"Well . . . so long."

"So long, Mr. Montgomery."

She swallowed hard as she watched him stride determinedly away from her and disappear around the side of the house. She didn't understand her sudden feeling of loneliness.

With a sigh, she let herself in the dark house and reached for the light switch. She had been right, the power was still off. Reaching for the candle and matches in the kitchen, she lit the wick and walked on through the dark house. She picked up stray litter here and there as she walked, and her arms were

61

soon filled. She nearly tripped over a large white sheet that had fallen off the cot they had put Martin on. Since her arms were full, she giggled and draped it over her head and laughed out loud as she thought of what Reed would say if he could see her now!

She suddenly jumped nervously as a loud pounding erupted at the front door. Reed had her as edgy as he was!

Her white sheet trailing eerily behind her, she walked to the door and held the candle up. "Who's there?"

"Me!"

"Reed?"

"Yeah, open the door."

Taryn reached down and unlocked the door and swung it open.

A loud gasp met her as Reed jumped back, his face turning ashen.

"Reed? What's wrong?"

"What do you think you're doing?" he asked weakly.

Taryn looked at him quizzically, then down at the flickering candle in her hand, and the sheet draped playfully over her head. "Oh"—she reached up and jerked the sheet off—"I was just straightening up a little bit. Did I frighten you?"

"Oh, hell, no. I'm used to ghosts answering the doors at funeral parlors," he scoffed.

"What's the matter? I thought you were leaving,"

Taryn asked as he brushed by her and stepped into the room.

"I was, but there's a twenty-foot tree lying across my car."

"Oh, that's too bad!" Taryn suddenly felt very happy once more. "I guess there's no one to remove it tonight, huh?" She tried very hard to keep the delight out of her voice.

"Not in this one-horse town," he grumbled.

"Well, the offer's still open to sleep here tonight."

"I was thinking that you might run me down to the nearest motel."

Taryn smiled serenely. "The 'nearest' motel is about seventy miles away, Reed. We don't even have a boardinghouse in Meadorville, let alone a Holiday Inn. I heard some people talking at the clinic and they said the full brunt of the storm hit over in the direction of the main highway, so undoubtedly it's impassable. I'm afraid you're stuck."

Reed looked defeated. "Then I guess I haven't any choice."

"You could always sleep in your car if you're afraid something's going to get you," she whispered in a low, ghostly tone of conspiracy.

"You think I haven't already thought of that? My Bronco happens to be packed full or that's exactly where I would be sleeping," he whispered back tersely.

Taryn laughed and supportively put her arm around his waist. "Come on, you big baby, I'll fix you

63

a bed on the sofa. I personally guarantee, barring an act of God, you'll still be safe and sound in the morning."

"Don't put me anywhere near that room . . . Martha's in," he warned in a whine.

"You don't want to be bunkies?"

"Cut the clowning, Taryn!"

"Such a baby," she clucked again, and affectionately squeezed his waist. For the life of her she didn't know why she was so glad to see this arrogant, cold-blooded lawyer, whose secret dream was to become a chicken farmer, back on her doorstep, but she was. That was what really worried her. She was not only glad, she was delighted.

CHAPTER FOUR

"Would you care for another slice of toast?" Taryn turned from the stove where she was frying bacon to confront a very haggard-looking Reed.

"No, thanks. I'll just have another cup of coffee, if you don't mind. Man alive! I don't feel like I've even been to bed," he confessed in a sleepy voice.

"That doesn't surprise me." Taryn's grin was mischievous as she lifted the crisp slices of bacon out on a paper towel to drain. "It couldn't be very relaxing to sleep with one eye open all night," she granted in a solemn voice.

"Both eyes open," he corrected earnestly as he polished off the last of his eggs and bacon.

"You sure you don't want more bacon or toast?" she prompted. She had gotten up early to make him a good breakfast and wanted him to stay as long as possible.

"Nope. As soon as I finish my coffee, I'm going to be on my way." As if to emphasize his words, he drained his cup and hurriedly set it back down on the table.

Taryn filled her plate and sat down at the table

opposite him in the sunny breakfast nook. Buttering her toast liberally, she bit into the crisp bread and idly wondered why the thought of his leaving disturbed her.

"What's the hurry?" she asked in a casual voice, trying to keep her tone impartial.

"I have to see about getting someone to get the tree off my car, and get it fixed as soon as possible. Elaine expects me in Santa Fe as soon as I can get there."

"Oh, yes. Elaine." Taryn forcefully attacked her eggs, trying to ignore the reference to Reed's fiancée. "As soon as I eat, I guess I better get busy myself," she confessed. "I have to see about getting the house put back in shape, then I'll go over and check on Grandpa."

"I hope the old fellow is doing okay," Reed offered.

"Oh, I'm sure he is. There's nothing 'old' about Grandpa," Taryn replied in a positive manner. "He'll bounce back in no time at all." She ate the last slice of bacon on her plate and hurriedly downed her orange juice. "I'd suggest you walk over to Hess's garage and see if Max can help you with your car. Ferris dropped by earlier this morning and told me Foster and his wife have been slightly injured in the storm, so he won't be able to help you."

"Who?"

"Foster. You know, the man who lives in the cottage out in back of the house. He and his wife help Grandpa run the funeral home."

66

"Oh, yeah. Well"—Reed stood up and stretched—"I suppose I should get started."

Taryn eyed with despair his rumpled clothes and the dark stubble on his face. "I'm sorry. I've forgotten my manners this morning. I'm sure you'll want to shower and change clothes before you leave," she proposed tactfully.

Absently rubbing the dark growth of his beard, he smiled self-consciously. "I hate to be a bother, but I do look rather disreputable, don't I?"

"A little," she agreed. "Why don't you go get your suitcase and shower and shave before you tackle the problem of your car," she suggested brightly as she rose from the table and walked over to the sink with their plates. "I'm sure Elaine wouldn't want you showing up in Santa Fe looking like an . . . opprobrious chicken farmer," she encouraged with a teasing grin.

"No, I'm sure she wouldn't want that, whatever that is," he acknowledged wryly.

"Not many women would," Taryn conceded, hating to allot Elaine any points in her favor, but after all, she knew *she* wouldn't want her intended showing up the way he looked right now! "The chicken farmer part wouldn't be so bad," she hastened to add, noting the look of distress on his face, "but I'm sure she would prefer you to look a little more . . . ." She searched frantically for a diplomatic description of what she thought Elaine would prefer. ". . . successful . . . maybe."

His laugh was deep and sincere and filled the room pleasantly. "Good try."

Taryn's shoulders lifted apologetically.

"I'll go get my suitcase," he chuckled, "and take you up on your very gracious offer."

"Good. Do you want me to walk you through the front part of the house?" she offered, knowing how uneasy he was in his present surroundings.

"No, thank you, I'm going out the back door."

"It's a lot farther," she reminded him.

"I need the exercise," he said quickly.

"Really? The way you've been racing through the front part of the house this morning, I would think exercise is the last thing you need," she teased him.

He opened the back door and saluted her in a cocky way. "In the words of someone famous: 'I shall return.'"

"In the words of someone not so famous, hurry up. We have a lot to do."

While he was gone, Taryn straightened the kitchen, thankful that this room had sustained the least damage. In fact, the entire living quarters had survived the main onslaught of the storm, with the exception of a few broken windows. Because of the storm, Martha Feagan's services would have to be postponed until the following day. Taryn was worried over the fact that for the next couple of weeks she would have to run the funeral home by herself until her grandfather recovered. Her concern wasn't over whether she could handle the responsibility.

68

She could, with her eyes closed. Although she had been gone a year, it didn't feel that long to her. It seemed like only yesterday she had left this town as a carefree bride, looking forward to a future filled with love. Little did she know she would be returning a mere twelve months later, alone.

A soft tap at the back door brought her abruptly back to the present as she called out for Reed to enter.

Minutes later she was ushering him to the bath off the main hallway and leaving a clean towel and a washcloth on the vanity. "If you need anything else, just yell," she instructed as she backed out of the small room.

"Thanks. I shouldn't be too long," he acknowledged gratefully.

Oh, dear Lord, *please* let him have a pair of trousers that don't make him look so darn *virile!* she prayed silently as she returned to her work.

She busied herself straightening up the family room and minutes later suddenly found herself softly singing along with the deep baritone voice coming from the shower in the bathroom. When she realized what she was doing, she paused and listened intently to Reed's voice drifting pleasantly through the air. He was unconsciously entertaining her with a popular ballad she had heard many times before, but never in the rich, soul-stirring way he was performing it.

When the bathroom door opened ten minutes

69

later, she was still marveling at how beautiful his voice was.

"It is amazing what a shower and shave can do for a person's morale," he conceded as he walked into the family room and set his suitcase down. "I actually feel human again."

Taryn's attention was drawn to his slacks, and she heaved an inward sigh of relief that her prayers had been answered. Although he looked stunningly handsome in his khaki slacks and polo shirt, they sufficiently disguised his impressive body.

"You smell good enough to attack," she teased, then caught herself in embarrassment. "I mean . . . you smell nice," she amended quickly.

"Attack, huh?" He hadn't let that unfortunate choice of words go unnoticed.

"You also have a very nice voice," she hurried on, hoping to distract him. "Do you sing professionally?"

"Attack, huh?" His grin was mischievous as he continued to pursue her slip of tongue. "Do you know something? It suddenly occurred to me I have never been attacked by a woman. Now that could prove interesting. I might want to give the idea some serious thought."

"Do you?"

"Yes, I've thought it over very carefully and you have my permission to attack me."

"No! I meant, do you sing professionally," she scolded, her face turning red at his teasing words.

"Do I sing professionally? Good grief, no! Where in the world would you get an idea like that?"

"I was listening to you sing while you were in the shower, and your voice is lovely," she said sincerely.

His face turned a miserable shade of pink now. "Could you hear me?"

Taryn nodded. "Martha and I both enjoyed it."

"Oh, come on. I had almost forgotten about . . . Martha," he groaned, not quite sure how to take her friendly badgering.

"Well, I can't forget Martha. I'm going to have to get busy and get the home back in shape for her services tomorrow. If you're ready, though, I'll walk to your car with you to see the damage myself. And since the phone is still out, I'll have to personally talk to Junior about getting the windows replaced."

"I'm ready," he acknowledged, picking up his suitcase. "I need to find a phone that's working and call Elaine and let her know I'm on my way."

"By all means," Taryn returned coolly. "She'll want to start whipping up her punch."

Forgetting for a moment Reed's aversion to his surroundings, Taryn led them through the front part of the house on the way outside. She noticed that Reed fell unusually silent and his eyes grew noticeably rounder as they passed the double wooden doors that were marked PARLOR A&B. A workman Taryn had visited and recruited earlier that morning was busy cleaning up the debris as she paused to talk to him.

71

"The man from the phone company said he'd have the phone back in commission by late this morning," the man told her as she stepped into the office and surveyed the progress being made.

"That's good to hear, Ronnie." Even though this was a very small town, a funeral director was on call twenty-four hours a day and a telephone was a necessity. "It looks like you're getting the bulk of things back in shape."

"I'm trying. You were real lucky, you know. The storm barely skimmed over this neighborhood, but the folks over on Wilder Street didn't fare as well."

Taryn frowned. "Was there a great deal of damage over there?"

"Afraid so. Tore down five whole blocks," he confirmed in a grim voice.

Taryn started straightening some papers on the desk. "We can be thankful there weren't any deaths, although I hear one man's injuries are still considered very serious." She glanced up and noticed Reed standing in the background as she chatted with the workman. "I'm sorry, Ronnie. I don't believe you've met Reed Montgomery."

Reed stepped forward and firmly grasped the older man's hand. "Hello, Ronnie. Nice to meet you."

"Reed was just passing through town when he was caught in the storm," Taryn explained. "I was just walking with him to his car."

"Then I won't keep you," Ronnie assured. He

72

reached for the broom he had been using and quietly went back to his work.

"This place doesn't look so bad in the light of day," Reed remarked casually as Taryn stepped out of the office and they began their journey once more.

"It isn't 'bad,'" she laughed. "Would you like me to show you around?"

"No . . . I don't have time. . . ." he refused swiftly.

"Oh, for heaven's sake. There isn't that much to see, actually." She reached over and took his hand and pulled him along beside her. "Now look. Over here we have the parlor." Pausing at the entrance of the elegantly furnished room, she let him survey the scene before him. "See. It's just a nice, quiet room that our families use for time alone to gather their thoughts," she explained, retracing their steps down the carpeted hallway. "We have four lovely slumber rooms, although we rarely use more than two."

"Slumber rooms?" Reed repeated in a weak voice.

"Yes, slumber rooms. Would you like to see one?" The look he shot her assured her he didn't.

"Martha is in . . . well, you know where Martha is," she said hastily, impatiently tugging at him as his footsteps faltered.

"Yes, I know where 'Martha' is, and it's my heart-felt desire she stay there . . . at least until I can get out of here," he grumbled.

All too soon, in Reed's opinion, they were standing

in front of another doorway, one that he immediately started backing away from.

"And here we have the preparation room," Taryn announced proudly. "Even though we are a very small business, Grandpa has always insisted on the most modern, up-to-date equipment for his home. . . . Reed! Get back here!" she demanded. "I'm not going to take you in there, I only wanted to point out where it was," she chided, firmly holding on to his hand, as if he were a child about to misbehave.

"I appreciate your time and consideration, but I think I've seen enough," he said in a determined voice, jerking his hand from hers almost belligerently. "I have to go."

"But you haven't seen our showroom," she protested in a small, disappointed voice. "There is the most gorgeous casket in there that you simply have to see. It has this yummy light-colored beige silk interior with a real innerspring mattress—"

"Taryn!"

"Yes?" She turned innocently to face him.

"No, I don't want to see a casket with an innerspring mattress!"

"Oh, you don't? Then how about the one with the water bed in it?" she tormented with a devilish glint in her eye.

"No! I don't want to see any of it!"

"Oh." She shrugged her shoulders and trailed along behind him as he stalked back through the hallway muttering something under his breath about getting out of this place before it got to him.

The morning sunlight was warm and exhilarating as Reed and Taryn stepped out the front door of the home and started their walk to his car.

"I love this time of year, don't you?" Taryn enthused, taking a deep, cleansing breath of the rainwashed summer air.

"It's all right," Reed muttered as she hurried along to keep up with his long strides. It was clear his mind was still back at the funeral home.

"Oh, you party pooper! Why are you so serious all the time?" Taryn reprimanded in a bubbly voice. She waved at an attractive, well-dressed, older couple walking on the other side of the street, calling out a friendly greeting to them.

"That's Lester and Elizabeth. They own the local market here in town, and they are two of the nicest people you'd ever want to meet. You want to meet them?" she queried hopefully. She didn't know why she was trying so hard to make him like her town, but she was. "You'd really like them," she promised.

"I haven't got time to meet them," he said firmly but politely. "I'm sure I would be crazy about them, but I have to take care of getting my car fixed and be on my way."

"Oh, well you just might be staying longer than you think and then you could help me . . . you know . . . until we see how Grandpa is going to be. . . ." Why had she opened her big mouth! Why, indeed, would he consider helping a strange woman who operated a business he was literally terrified of? But she plunged on anyway. "You know, you might not be able to get anyone to cut the tree off your car today and you really don't know how badly damaged it is," she warned, hurrying to catch up with him as he started walking again, and at a much faster pace than he had before, she noticed. "Everyone's busier than a long-tailed cat in a roomful of rockers. It took me a while this morning to round up someone to clean the mortuary."

"If I have to chew the tree off my car, I'll do it," he said matter-of-factly. By now they had reached the car, which he grimly surveyed. "Elaine is not the most patient person in the world," he added as an afterthought.

"Well, it's quite possible that she may have to develop that characteristic," Taryn returned, her voice showing annoyance for the first time.

"It's also quite possible that she won't," he pointed out blandly.

"You still have six days before the wedding takes place."

"Six days? Yeah, I guess it is only six days away now." For a moment it sounded like the idea had unexpectedly sneaked up on him. "But that doesn't matter. I have to get there as soon as I can."

Taryn seethed inwardly as he walked around the blue Ford Bronco, quietly assessing his chances of getting an early start out of town this morning.

He sounded as if his precious Elaine had brain-washed him, she thought, simmering irritably. Taryn bade him a cool good-bye and started on down the street, leaving him alone with his troubled car, his misguided forthcoming marriage, and hopeless dreams of a chicken ranch he would never have.

It took most of the morning for her to arrange for the windows to be repaired, and to visit with her grandpa, who was doing remarkably well. Assuring him again that she would have no problem running the business by herself until he could take part once more, she returned home and ate a light lunch, then went upstairs to take a short nap.

As she lay across her bed, she reached for the small photograph on her bedside table of a smiling, blond-haired man with laughing blue eyes. Rolling over on her back, she hugged the picture close to her heart and desperately tried to remember the smell and feel of Gary. She hadn't wanted to forget the smallest detail about him, but it was growing harder every day to recall even the simplest things about him, like what shade of blue his eyes were, or was his hair really blond or just slightly golden? Every night, she would fall asleep staring at his picture trying to re-new her memory, but an old photograph was a poor substitute for a pair of strong arms to hold her through the long, lonely nights.

"Oh, Gary," she murmured. "Why did you have to go?" She sighed once more, and propped up on her elbow. A terrible sense of loneliness crept over her.

"Oh, Gary. I wish you were here with me," she whispered in a muffled sob as her eyes drifted shut in weariness. "When will the pain ever stop?"

She couldn't have dozed for more than a few minutes before she heard the peal of the front-door chimes. Trying to overcome the drowsiness that held her captive, she struggled off the bed and stumbled downstairs. Someone must be coming to check about Martha's services, she speculated sleepily. Ronnie had told her there had been a steady stream of people dropping by this morning, while she had been out, to ask about the new arrangements.

When she opened the door and found Reed Montgomery standing there, a thrill of elation shot through her before she quickly covered her delight and made herself comment in a blasé tone, "Why, hello. Are we slumming again?"

" 'We' still have a tree on our car," he lamented in a miserable voice saturated with defeat.

"How heartbreaking! Couldn't you manage to chew it off?" She was trying her darndest to keep the elation out of her voice.

"No, but I tried," he solemnly hastened to add. "But you were right. It looks like I'm going to be stuck here. I've covered every square inch of this town looking for an available man to clear the tree off my car, and there just isn't any. Say," he asked, suddenly coming up with a hopeful solution, "you don't happen to have a chain saw I could use, do you?"

"No." She sighed in mock resignation. "Contrary

78

to what you've seen in old horror movies, we don't use chain saws in our business anymore."

His face turned a shade paler. "Will you cut that out!"

"Oh, all right," she relented crossly. This guy was something else! "I assume you have chosen to grace my doorstep again for some reason. To what do I owe the honor?"

"Now, look. If you weren't looking at a desperate man, I wouldn't be within two hundred miles of this place right now, but the way I see it, I don't have a whole lot of alternatives. There isn't a room available anywhere, my car isn't going anywhere, not to mention the fact that all of the highways leading out of town are blocked with fallen power lines, so what am I gonna do!"

"So, you're 'gonna' have to stay here again tonight," she stated simply, her pulse racing at the unexpected but highly welcome prospect.

"I suppose I will," he returned glumly. "I don't want to seem ungrateful but—"

"You don't have to sleep downstairs again. You can use Grandpa's room," she offered, trying to make the sleeping arrangements a little more palatable for him. "I don't know why I didn't think of that last night."

A look of pathetic relief invaded his features now. "Thanks, I really would appreciate that."

Reed was about to step through the open door

when Taryn heard a woman's voice breathlessly calling out to him.

Reed turned and watched as Sadie Mullins came scurrying up on the porch, carrying Malcolm in his birdcage.

"Oh, I'm so glad I caught you," she gasped. "Malcolm would have never forgiven me if I had left him with anyone else while I was gone!"

Both Reed and Taryn stared wordlessly at the squawking bird swinging back and forth on his perch. "Are you going somewhere?" Taryn finally asked.

"I have to check into the clinic for a few days," she moaned. "I have a heart condition and with all the excitement I'm afraid it's decided to act up again. I know this is asking an awful lot of you, but Martin always told me to call on him if I needed anything. . . . Oh, I hate to be such a bother, but I don't have anyone to watch Malcolm and then I remembered how firm Mr. Montgomery was with him the night of the storm and I just knew he would be the one to watch him while I was in the clinic. Even though Malcolm acts as if he doesn't like Mr. Montgomery, I'm quite sure he does! I'm afraid Malcolm has become a little unruly since my husband died and he needs a good firm hand!" she admitted candidly.

Reed glanced helplessly at Taryn, silently willing her to get him out of this mess. "Uh . . . oh, boy . . . I'm afraid I'm in a bad position to watch your bird right now, Sadie . . . I've got to—"

Malcolm let out an ear-piercing squawk, followed by a round of violent swinging on his perch as he yelled over and over, "Malcolm is a baaad boy! Malcolm is a baaad boy!"

"No, no dear. The nice man didn't say you were a bad boy!" Sadie crooned, trying to console the frantically swinging bird. She cast an apologetic look in Taryn and Reed's direction. "He's such a sensitive little darling. I shouldn't have said what I did about him getting out of hand since Lonnie died. . . ."

"Squawk! Malcolm wants Poppy!" the bird demanded in a belligerent voice.

"Oh, dear me, now I've got him thinking about Poppy again, that's what he called my husband," she explained with a wail, hovering close to tears herself now.

Taryn hastily took the birdcage out of her hand and thrust it toward Reed. "We'll take care of Malcolm," she promised, ignoring the look of "wait till I get my hands on you!" he had shot her. "Reed may be too busy trying to get his car fixed, but I'll take good care of your bird."

"Oh, would you?" Sadie's tears ceased instantly as she smiled at Reed, who was now tapping on the side of the birdcage, irritably trying to assert his authority over the unruly bird.

"You know, he isn't really a bird," she confessed. "He's more like the child I never had."

Taryn smiled tolerantly. "You go on to the clinic and don't worry about a thing."

81

"Would you water my plants and feed my other pets while I'm gone?" she asked hopefully. "Malcolm is the only one who needs personal attention at all times."

"Just leave me a key and I'll take care of everything," Taryn promised.

Minutes later, after a round of loud, squawking good-byes from Malcolm, Sadie was on her way, assured that everything she loved would still be intact when she returned home in a few days.

"I can't *believe* you agreed to keep this loudmouth for two days!" Reed groaned, jerking his finger back from the cage moments before Malcolm could take a hunk of skin. "This bird hates me!"

"You're imagining things," Taryn excused, uneasily eyeing the bird from a distance. "Didn't you hear Sadie say he secretly liked you?"

He turned his eyes up toward the heavens in a desperate plea. "What have I done to deserve this?" he beseeched. "Don't you think a redheaded mortician and a psychopathic bird are a little severe?"

"Squawk! Malcolm is a baaad boy! Malcolm is a baaad boy!" the bird shouted.

"He sure *is!* Squawk! He sure *is!*" Reed parroted in disgusted agreement.

The sound of Taryn's laughter followed him as he entered the house and hastily went in search of somewhere to put his new charge.

CHAPTER FIVE

"You look sleepy this morning."

"I *am* sleepy this morning," Reed confirmed in a grouchy voice the next day at breakfast. "That darn bird talked all night."

"About what?"

"Who knows! I'm telling you, Taryn, that bird needs some kind of therapy. He's got the worst inferiority complex I've ever encountered! When he wasn't jabbering about wanting something to eat, he was shouting 'Malcolm is a baaad boy' all night long."

Taryn got up to pour more coffee for them, silently noting that two nights of disrupted sleep was leaving its mark on him. They had had an early supper the evening before and both had retired to their rooms, hoping to catch up on their rest. Apparently, Reed's effort had failed.

"You can put Malcolm in my room tonight," she offered.

"I hope I won't have to," he pointed out. "I've got to call Elaine again," he murmured to himself.

"Instead of promising her you'll be there a certain

day, why don't you simply tell her you'll be there as soon as you can?"

"I've told her that every time I've called."

"Does she know where you are? Where you're staying?"

"She knows I'm stranded in a town named Meadorville, but she doesn't know exactly where I'm staying," he hedged.

"Well, it's all very innocent," Taryn reminded casually. It disturbed her when she thought of his marrying Elaine, especially the reason he was marrying her for. She didn't know why she felt so protective of him, but it just seemed to her he deserved much better in life. A marriage without love would, in Taryn's opinion, be unbearable.

"Are you sure you really want to go through with this marriage?" she asked him gently.

Instead of surprised indignation, which she fully expected, his answer was quiet and pensive. "There're times I have doubts about it," he confessed. "I thought that went along with the game."

"Game?" Taryn shook her head sadly. "Marriage and love aren't a game, Reed."

"Love!" He voiced the word musingly. "I don't see what the big fuss is. I've seen the earth-shattering kind portrayed in movies and I read about it in almost every book I pick up, every song I hear on the radio, but personally I think it's all a lot of malarkey."

"You've never been in love?" she asked him incredulously.

"Not that way," he confided. "Oh, I love my family.
. . ."

"But you've never loved a woman with all those 'earth-shattering' feelings you just spoke about? You've never met anyone you just *knew* you didn't want to live without?"

"No, I haven't." His gaze was fixed steadily on his cup as he spoke calmly. "I just told you, I don't believe in that kind of love."

"Boy, are you in for a surprise," she remarked playfully.

"Did you and your husband have that kind of love?"

"You bet we did," she said honestly. "And I have every intention of finding it again someday."

"Well, as I've told you before, Elaine and I will have a good marriage without all that . . . togetherness." He pushed away from the table, stood up, and stretched. "I guess I better go feed Malcolm. He was sleeping like a rock when I left the room this morning."

Taryn laughed. "He was probably exhausted from his night of chatter."

"What's on your agenda today?" he inquired pleasantly as they walked out of the kitchen.

"Martha Feagan's services are this afternoon. I have a world of things to do before then. You don't suppose you could help me with some of them, do you? Foster isn't feeling very well this morning. He

85

won't be here to help me until this afternoon. He'll have to drive the hearse to the cemetery for me."

"I can't, Taryn. . . ." Reed hated to refuse her after all she had done for him, yet he couldn't bring himself to offer his help. It would have been a different case altogether if she worked in maybe a restaurant or something. He'd be glad to fry hamburgers or scrub floors to help her out, but a mortuary . . . He shuddered. "I should start looking for someone to cut that tree off my Bronco."

"All I want you to do is run the sweeper in the front foyer for me," she chided, knowing exactly why he was refusing.

"Just run the sweeper?"

"That's all. I have a lot of paperwork I have to do and I have to be sure I have all the cards off the floral arrangements. You could do that if you'd rather," she offered, forgetting his allergies for a moment.

"Where are the flowers?" he asked cautiously.

"Well . . . you know . . . in there with Martha."

"I'll sweep." He made his choice without a second thought. "Where's the sweeper?"

"In the storage closet. Come on, I'll show you."

She hustled him down the hallway and stopped before a large door that housed the mops, brooms, sweeper, and cleaning supplies. "If you don't mind, could you dust a little, too?"

"Now wait a minute," he grumbled, dragging the large, heavy-duty sweeper out of the closet. "I thought I was only supposed to run the sweeper in the foyer."

"Well, for heaven's sake! While you have it out, it's not going to hurt you to run it in the parlor, too. You wouldn't want people to come to a dusty funeral, would you?"

"Who in the world is going to notice a little bit of dust if they're coming to a funeral?" he asked in disbelief. "That's the last thing I'd have on my mind! Besides, I've already done all I can for Martha. I picked her up and put her back in that thing after the storm, didn't I?"

"I bet you don't attend funerals, period, do you?" she surmised correctly. "I bet you just let your friends leave this world without so much as a 'so long, it's been good to know you,'" she finished irritably, plugging in the sweeper and handing it to him.

"If they're *my* friends, I guarantee they're not even looking for me," he answered serenely.

"Sweep the office while you're at it." Taryn gave him a dirty look and walked away, seething at his indifference to mankind.

Reed tackled the parlor first and had it shining in thirty minutes. He carefully avoided the area where he knew the two double doors were closed, saving it until last. When he could no longer put it off, he dragged his cleaning supplies and sweeper over to Parlor B and set to work.

He was whistling under his breath, trying to keep his mind off what he knew lay on the other side of the wooden doors, when he looked up and saw the doors opening. He paused in his work, his eyes narrowing suspiciously as a large, stern-faced woman walked toward him. He had no idea who she was and he wasn't quite sure if he really wanted to.

"Pardon me," she summoned in an authoritative voice, "I was wondering if you could help me."

Reed paused, letting his sweeper run as he looked her over cautiously. What was she doing in Martha's room? The vacuum sounded as if it were sucking up rocks now as Reed leaned closer and asked in a wary voice, "What did you say?"

The woman took a deep, offensive breath, drawing in her mammoth bosom. "I said, I need your help!"

Still unable to make out her words above the clatter of the sweeper, Reed reached down and shut it off. "Now, what did you say?"

"Are you deaf?" she asked, none too kindly. "Must you respond in such a boisterous refrain? You *are* aware that there are those reposing in this house!"

"I am aware of that," he said, relenting. "Who are you?"

"I am Ms. Feagan!"

Reed's stubborn features went instantly limp. He sagged against the sweeper and stared at her with a sheepish grin on his face. "You are not," he accused weakly.

"I most certainly am!"

"No, you're not!" he insisted stubbornly, still exhibiting a disbelieving, shaky grin. "Mrs. Feagan is re-

posing. . . . I know she is. I helped put her there.
. . ."

"Young man, just who do you think you are?"

"Lady! I know who I am. You cut out the clowning
and tell me who you are," he said in a cross voice.

"I told you, I'm Ms. Feagan and my gladiolus are
dry. What are you going to do about it?" Her black,
beady eyes pinned him to the spot, demanding a
prompt and immediate answer.

"I'm not going to do anything about . . . that," he
hedged dogmatically, not having the slightest idea of
what a gladiolus was or what to do about it. "Taryn
takes care of . . . you reposing people. You'll have
to go ask her." He had no idea who this woman was,
but if she thought she was Martha Feagan, he wasn't
going to stand here trying to convince her she wasn't.

At the sound of loud, angry voices coming from the
hallway, Taryn stuck her head out of the doorway
and glanced toward Parlor B. "Millicent? Is there
something wrong?" she called softly.

The woman and Reed were squared off facing each
other like two combatants as Taryn hurriedly slipped
out of the office and came over to where they were
standing. "Is there a problem?" she asked.

"This brash young man *will not* get any water for
the gladiolus I sent Mother yesterday," Millicent Feagan cried in a heartbroken voice. "It breaks my heart
to see those lovely blooms growing more wilted every minute."

"Reed?" Taryn glanced at him in puzzlement as

she slipped her arm through his and separated the warring factions. "Why wouldn't you get Millicent some water for her mother's flowers?"

"She told me she *was* Martha Feagan!" he tattled in a distraught voice.

"I did not tell him I was Mother!" Millicent gasped, her face turning as pale as Reed's now. "I told him I was Ms. Feagan!"

"That's what I said!" he bellowed. "You told me your name was Feagan!"

"My name *is* Feagan, you idiot!" she bellowed in a most unladylike voice.

"Quiet, you two!" Taryn hissed under her breath. "Now this is ridiculous! Reed, this is Martha's daughter, Millicent. Now please go get her a pitcher of water so she can take care of the flowers." She turned to place a placating arm around the sniffling woman. "Now, please try to pull yourself together, Millicent. This has all been just a small misunderstanding. Reed didn't know that you were Martha's daughter and he's been a little edgy today," she comforted, shooting Reed a murderous glare.

"He was so rude," she whimpered self-righteously. "He didn't care one whit whether Mother's gladiolus went limp!"

"Oh, no, Millicent, he cares," Taryn crooned, leading her back through the wooden double doors. "He's really very understanding."

"See, I told you you weren't Mrs. Feagan," he gloated childishly under his breath as Millicent passed him. He was smugly determined to have the last word in this argument.

"Reed!" Taryn scolded heatedly. "Go get the water!"

"I'm going already!" He turned and marched irritably toward the kitchen.

When he returned, he set the water down in front of the doors of Parlor B and yelled for Millicent to "Come and get it!" then went straight to the office and loudly slammed the door. Minutes later, Taryn followed, closing the door quietly behind her. "That little scene was completely uncalled-for, Reed. We are trying to operate this business in a quiet, dignified manner and that does not include yelling 'Come and get it!' in our slumber rooms and slamming office doors."

"Don't start with me, Taryn," he warned in a testy voice. "You know how this place gets to me! I'm out there minding my own business when this lunatic looking like a marine drill sergeant comes waltzing out of Parlor B and announces she is Ms. Feagan! What in the hell was I supposed to do? Believe her?"

Taryn stifled a laugh, determined to keep a straight face in front of him. She was aware he was nervous in his new surroundings and she had to be tolerant with him. "I still think you could have been politer. After all, she is a customer, and her name is Ms. Feagan. She's never married."

"No kidding," he mocked. "I wonder why?"

"Reed." Taryn frowned at his lack of tact.

"Is this phone working yet?" He eyed the receiver hopefully.

"Yes, why—"

"I'm going to call Elaine."

Taryn's heart fell. "Oh, do you want me to leave?" She was beginning to notice a disconcerting pattern. Every time things got tough, he had to call his precious Elaine!

"Suit yourself, I'm not going to seduce her over the telephone," he assured her in a grumpy voice. Picking up the receiver, he dialed the long-distance operator and placed a collect call to Elaine Matthews in Santa Fe, New Mexico.

Taryn busied herself with the paperwork she had been working on earlier as he talked with his fiancée. Although he was being very casual in his conversation, Taryn felt stirrings of jealousy toward Elaine. He was talking to the woman he was going to be marrying in another few days! Berating herself for such foolish feelings, she tried to block out Reed's voice and was surprised at how successful she was. It shouldn't make any difference one way or the other whom he was talking to, or in what manner he was talking to them, she reminded herself. But, darn it, it did!

"How many times are you going to staple that piece of paper," she heard his voice ask a few minutes later.

Looking up from her work, she encountered Reed's amused face. "What?"

"The paper. How many times are you going to staple it?" he repeated patiently, motioning to the social security form she had absently riddled with staples.

Taryn stared blankly at the paper in her hand, then threw it back on the desk in embarrassment. "I like to be sure none of the forms are lost," she excused lamely. "Saves me a lot of trouble."

"It might save you a lot of trouble," he agreed, "but I'd sure hate to be the one you're sending it to."

"Well, you're not, so why worry? How's Elaine?" Taryn stood up and walked over to file the paper, hoping he didn't think she had been listening to his conversation and not concentrating on her work.

"She's a little ticked off, but she'll get over it." Taryn detected a strained optimism in his answer.

"Still doesn't understand your situation?" she queried lightly. "Would it help if I called her and explained?"

"I hope you're joking," he said.

Taryn shut the file cabinet and smiled innocently. "Why, no. Should I be?" She exaggeratedly batted her eyelashes at him.

Leaning back in the chair he was seated in, he propped his feet on the desk and lit a cigarette. Through a haze of smoke his eyes narrowed appreciably as he seemed suddenly to take a candid and admiring look at her for the first time. "Let's put it this way. How would you feel if your fiancé was holed up somewhere with a redhead who was built like

93

Raquel Welch, and that same fiancé happens to have a terrible weakness when it comes to redheads with big hazel eyes, skin like peaches and cream, a fanny that's. . . ." His voice trailed off sexily as his eyes continued to lazily explore the outlines of her thin cotton dress. ". . . that's very hard to keep his hands off."

Mixed feelings of pleasure surged through her as she made her way back over to the desk and sank down in her chair. Her heart hammered painfully against her ribs and she wondered where all the air in the room had suddenly disappeared to.

"I wasn't aware you were attracted . . . to redheads," she stammered softly, hoping he wasn't playing some silly little macho game with her.

"Come now, Taryn. Let's not play coy," he chided. "You know you're a darn attractive woman."

"I'm not being 'coy,'" she protested, trying to avoid the smoldering invitation in his gray eyes. "You haven't given me one indication you felt attracted to me."

He took a long drag off his cigarette, letting the smoke curl out in tiny little ringlets, still intently studying her. "I haven't? What do you call that kiss we shared a couple of nights ago."

She laughed in a shaky voice. "For me? Desperation! I haven't been kissed by a man in over a year and I guess I went bananas for a minute."

"Desperate widow, huh?" His smile was wicked. "Sounds interesting."

94

"Not that desperate," she cautioned. "Are you playing little games with me, Mr. Montgomery? Because if you are, you're wasting your time. I've made it well over a year without the companionship of a man and I haven't any plans to change my state of celibacy."

"I'm not doing anything other than sitting here smoking a cigarette," he denied in an innocent voice. "You're reading something into the conversation that isn't there, desperate widow." He winked innocently.

Taryn smiled tolerantly. "Of course. I'm so sorry for misjudging you. I'm sure you're a perfect angel."

"Maybe not perfect, but close to it," he agreed, sitting up straighter to stub his cigarette out in the ashtray. "What do you want me to do next?"

Taryn looked at him warily. "In relation to what?"

"In relation to my cleaning duties." He had changed the subject so quickly, she was taken off guard.

"My goodness. You scared me for a minute," she said, laughing. "I thought we were still talking about me." She couldn't help feeling a slight disappointment that he had given up so easily.

For a moment his gaze captured hers and held it. "I think we'd better change the subject before I start saying things a man engaged shouldn't be saying to another woman," he said matter-of-factly.

"If a man feels like he wants to say 'things' to another woman, maybe he shouldn't be engaged at all," she reminded him, reaching out to gently touch his hand. She didn't know what had gotten into her lately. She had never made a pass at a man who was engaged!

His hand closed over hers in mutual understanding as they stood facing each other in the small room. His touch sent shivers of delight racing down her spine, and for a moment she considered leaning over, wrapping her arms around his neck, and kissing him senseless! At that moment, there was nothing in the world she wanted more!

"Maybe he shouldn't," Reed relented in a voice suddenly filled with seriousness. He reached out to touch a lock of her hair reverently. "The color of your hair reminds me of the sun setting on a hot summer evening," he whispered huskily.

"Can I kiss you?" she asked impetuously, no longer able to deny her attraction to him.

By the sudden look of shock on Reed's face, you would have thought she had asked if she could pull his toenails out by the roots! "No!" he refused guiltily. He drew away quickly and fumbled nervously in his shirt pocket for another cigarette.

"Why not?" she demanded, a shadow of annoyance flickering across her face. He didn't love Elaine! He had admitted as much!

"Because, damn it, I'm engaged!" he told her in exasperation.

"That doesn't count because you don't really love Elaine," Taryn pointed out, stepping closer to his lithe, muscular physique. "If I really thought for one minute that you loved her, I wouldn't dream of doing what I'm about to do. You don't need that cigarette!" She snatched it out of his hand and threw it into the waste can.

"Have a heart, Taryn," he pleaded, warily backing away from her. But she persisted and, as her arms went up around his neck and she buried her fingers in the thick dark waves she had been powerless to take her eyes off, the fight slowly began to drain out of him. Sensing her victory, her mouth feather-touched his in flagrant seduction.

"This is miserable . . . you're supposed to respect my state of engagement. . . ."

"That's just what your engagement is—a miserable state. How long is it going to take for you to realize it?" Her mouth came down softly on his and she kissed him in a most aggressive manner. At first he obediently avoided the onslaught, but seconds later he was kissing her with a hunger that belied his indifference. Pulling her toward him, he molded their bodies closer and closer as his mouth devoured the sweetness of hers, breaking away only occasionally to catch a short, ragged breath. Taryn had no idea why she was torturing herself like this . . . their relationship could never go anywhere. But for the moment it didn't matter. She simply didn't care. He felt so good pressed against her softness, he tasted so good, he smelled so good. . . .

She knew she should protest when he began to

caress her bottom intimately, running his large hands over the delightful dips and curves as his tongue scrimmaged sensuously with hers. "It feels as good as I thought it would," he confessed with a wry grin. "Now I'm going to want to know how it feels without all this material wrapped around it." Taryn grew weak as he nipped at the corners of her mouth and pressed her tighter against his rising desire. "Don't you?"

"I know what it feels like," she said inanely, letting him have better access to her neck with his moist, warm kisses.

"Yeah . . . but I don't. We could change all that if you want to take a few minutes off from your work. . . ."

If a knock hadn't sounded on the office door then, Taryn didn't honestly know what her answer would have been. It would have been very tempting to let him find out for himself! The interruption sent them repentantly scampering apart from each other, yet it was several moments later before Taryn could manage a shaky "Come in."

Millicent Feagan stuck her head in the doorway and frowned when she saw Reed standing there. "May I have a word with you?" she asked Taryn.

"Of course." Taryn straightened her dress and hurriedly brushed by Reed. "Why don't you go fix us a sandwich?" she murmured. "We'll just have time to eat before Martha's service begins."

"All right. I'll meet you in the kitchen." She noticed his voice wasn't exactly steady as a rock either.

Millicent's problem could turn out to be a big one and Taryn was still thinking about it when she joined Reed in the kitchen ten minutes later.

"What's old picklepuss's problem this time?" Reed asked sourly, still ticked off over his earlier encounter with Martha Feagan's old-maid daughter.

"She's concerned because the singer for Martha's services hasn't shown up yet."

"Let *her* get up there and belt out a song," Reed suggested, slapping ham and cheese between slices of whole wheat bread. "That should put a little life in the service."

"Reed! That isn't funny! I could have a serious problem on my hands," Taryn admonished.

They ate their sandwiches in silence, neither attempting conversation. Taryn berated herself for acting in such a love-starved, asinine way earlier. She had no doubt that she had scared Reed to death with her blatant aggression. Even though he had responded, she still had no right to make a play for another woman's fiancé. She made a mental note to control herself in the future.

Reed said very little during the meal, asking for the pepper once and the salt twice. They both seemed relieved when the meal was over and Taryn took their plates to the sink.

"I'll just have time to freshen my makeup before

99

the service starts. What are you going to do this afternoon?"

"Try to get something done about my car," he returned curtly.

"Well, that's going to take some time and even if your car was all right, you wouldn't be able to leave," she pointed out. "The highways are still impassable."

"I know, but those highways have to be reopened before long and I want to be sitting there with my motor idling when they do." For the first time since their passionate encounter in the office, he looked directly at her, his silvery gray eyes growing cloudy. "I . . . have to leave, surely you realize that," he reiterated in a strained voice.

"Yes, I know you think you do." Taryn swallowed hard and refused to look at him. "I'll only be a few minutes."

When she emerged from the bathroom five minutes later, Reed was waiting for her. Silently, they walked down the hallway, both wrapped in their own thoughts.

"Oh, shoot. I forgot to feed Malcolm." Reed's footsteps faltered as they neared the small chapel where people were already somberly filing in, in honor of Martha Feagan. "I better run back up and see about him. He didn't eat much of his breakfast."

Taryn was a bit surprised at Reed's concern for Malcolm. "How much is a parrot supposed to eat?"

"I have no idea, but I noticed he just sort of pecked

around at his food this morning," Reed fretted. "I wouldn't want Sadie to come back and find him sick."

"Well, I confess I know nothing about parrots, but I don't think his pecking at his food is anything to be concerned over. I'm sure he isn't going to sit down and eat his birdseed with a knife, fork, and spoon."

"I still better go check on him. I'll slip out the back door so I won't disturb the services," he promised. Before Taryn could make any further comment, he had turned and disappeared back down the hallway.

Ten minutes later Taryn burst into the family quarters, frantically calling his name. "Reed! Where are you?" If he had already left, she didn't know what she would do!

The bedroom door flew open and Reed rushed out clutching a box of birdseed in his hand, his face a mask of anxiety. "What's wrong?"

"It's Martha! It's Martha!" she gulped, trying to catch her breath.

Reed's face turned an ashen gray. "Again? What's wrong with her now?" His eyes narrowed suspiciously. "So help me, Taryn, if she's fallen out of her casket again, she can just climb back in herself because I'm *not*—"

"*She* didn't do anything, you ninny! But the man who was supposed to sing at her service never showed up!" Taryn interrupted.

Sagging weakly against the couch, Reed tried to steady his frayed nerves. "Is that all! Well, put on a record! And *please* stop running through this damn

101

house yelling 'It's Martha! It's Martha!' I will never be so *glad* to see a woman go to her final resting place *and* stay there!" he bellowed angrily.

"This is serious, Reed," Taryn said. "You are simply going to *have* to help me this time."

"No way," he stated bluntly. *"No way!"*

"Can you read music?" She totally ignored his growing case of hysterics.

"I refuse to answer on the grounds it might incriminate me," he said, crossing his arms stubbornly.

"Ah hah! I knew it. You can read music, can't you?"

"Very little," he snapped in a belligerent tone.

"Can you play any kind of an instrument?"

"The harp, and I do a little ballet, but I didn't pack my tights!"

"Come on, Reed! Be serious! I have a whole chapel of people sitting out there waiting for a service that was supposed to begin ten minutes ago. *You have to help me!*" she demanded in a panic-stricken voice.

Reed's face sagged in defeat. "Oh, bull! All right. I know how to play the piano! But I wouldn't if my mother hadn't made me when I was a kid," he defended himself meekly.

"Oh, thank goodness!" Taryn's voice was full of relief. "Okay. I'll play the organ and you can play the piano. Do you read music well enough to play a duet with me?"

Reed's shoulders lifted indifferently. "I took lessons for eight long miserable years."

"Oh, good, oh, good;" she murmured in a relieved

tone. "I know you can sing like a lark, so we'll both play the duet and then you can sing a couple of verses of the song Martha requested, 'When They Ring Those Golden Bells.' You do know, 'When They Ring Those Golden Bells'?"

Reed's face was mirroring shock, then disbelief, as she rattled off her hasty instructions.

"Reed! Answer me. Do you know 'When They Ring Those Golden Bells'?" she persisted.

"No, I don't know 'When They Ring Them Golden Bells,' and even if I did, there's no way in the world I'm going to go out there and sing in front of all those people!"

"Oh, pooh! You really have a much nicer voice than the man who was supposed to sing in the first place," Taryn dismissed airily. "Okay, you can sing 'The Old Rugged Cross.' Surely you know that one. Everyone in the world knows that song!" she accused.

"Of course I know 'The Old Rugged Cross', but I'm not going to sing it! It's your funeral home, *you* sing it!"

"I can't sing!" she wailed. "My voice sounds like someone running their fingernails down a chalkboard! You will have to sing it, hum it, whistle it . . . I don't care. Just help me get through this catastrophe!"

"I absolutely refuse." He planted his feet solidly on the floor and stared at her in defiance. "Period. Subject closed."

"Oh, no, it isn't!" Taryn grabbed his arm and

103

started physically dragging him out the door. "You can't let me down now and I don't have time to stand here and argue with you," she fumed. "If you don't do this for me, I'll call Elaine and tell her where you are, and that you've been staying in a house with a desperate young widowed redhead the last two nights!"

"You wouldn't dare!" he bellowed, dragging his heels down the hallway. "You don't know how to get in touch with her!"

"If you don't get out there and sing, you just watch me! I can pick up the phone and place a collect call to Elaine Matthews in Santa Fe, New Mexico, just as easily as you can!"

"Let go, Taryn, I mean it! Let go!" he stormed, trying to jerk his arm loose from her stranglehold. "I'm not going out there!" he yelled as she pulled him along the empty corridor, stringing the boxful of birdseed he was carrying all over the carpet he had vacuumed earlier. *I mean it, you crazy redhead, I won't do it!*

CHAPTER SIX

At any other time, their entrance into the small cubicle that housed the organ and piano for Lassiter Funeral Home would have been nothing short of disgraceful, but Taryn's only concern at the moment was getting the "guest" singer into position. The service should have started a full fifteen minutes earlier and she simply couldn't delay any longer.

The rustle of papers and the heated whispers could be heard in the small, quiet chapel as the mourners turned their eyes in the direction of the sheer curtain and watched with bated expectation.

"Sit down over there and be quiet," Taryn hissed as she frantically shuffled through the music looking for the piano-organ duet she had performed many times before in this chapel.

"I'm *not* going to do it," Reed vowed in a pleading whisper. "I've never sung before anyone in my whole life, and besides, I'll sneeze my brains out around all those flowers!"

"This room is far enough away from the flowers so you shouldn't have any trouble," Taryn dismissed irritably. The pile of music in her lap slid off onto the floor as they continued to argue. "Now look what you've made me do," she jeered impatiently.

"Oh, good grief! Let me do it and let's get this insanity over with!" They both reached to retrieve the fallen music at the same time, their heads banging painfully into each other with a loud crack. They both saw stars for a full sixty seconds before Reed staggered over to the piano bench, bellowing in excruciating pain.

"Oh, damn! You've cracked my head open," he screamed in an agonized whisper.

"Me!" Taryn gingerly rubbed her head, tears smarting her eyes. "I'm not wearing this three-inch knot because it's the latest style, you know! Now shut up and take this music!" She threw a sheet of music at him and hit the first note on the organ loudly.

Every guest in the chapel jumped a good two inches out of their seats as the music blared over the intercom, signaling that the service had finally begun.

The sweet, melodious sound of the organ filled the chapel as Taryn began to play the opening refrain of a beautiful hymn, one that immediately stirred the hearts of the mourners. For several minutes she played flawlessly, watching Reed uneasily from the corner of her eye. He sat on the piano bench rubbing his head, shooting her poisonous glares. She could tell he was quietly assessing his chances of her bluffing about calling Elaine. This was the duet he had agreed to play—not sing—so she didn't have any worries yet, she told herself as her fingers moved professionally over the keys. The real test would come later when the duet was over.

When she came to the part that called for the piano solo, she held her breath and glanced in Reed's direction. Without a moment's hesitation, the sound of the piano rang out clearly and exquisitely in the hushed chapel as he played the notes of the music with an expertise that astounded her. Tiny goose bumps popped out all over her as the music swelled and filled the air with heavenly glory as the listeners were asked to "abide with me" in the most soul-stirring way Taryn had ever heard it played. His fingers moved effortlessly over the ivory keys, and only the look of strained concentration on his face reminded her he was performing under extreme coercion. Together, the organ and piano joined in harmony, and before the song was through, tears of emotion were slipping quietly down Taryn's face. She glanced sheepishly over at Reed, and her tears ceased instantly when she noticed he was glaring at her as if she had lost all her marbles this time!

"What's wrong now?" he mouthed crossly. "Did I hit a sour note?"

She waved his question away with her hand and hastily shuffled through her music once more, looking for "The Old Rugged Cross." Men! How could they be so sensitive one minute and so callous the next! She thrust his copy of the sheet music to him, and watched as he glanced at the title for a second, then began shaking his head adamantly.

Pointing her finger at him, as a parent would do to a disobedient child, she nodded her head firmly and mutinously hit the opening note on the organ.

In deliberate rebellion, Reed crossed his arms, then crossed his legs, and calmly shook his head vigorously.

Again, a little louder this time, Taryn hit the note, trying to glare him into submission.

The guests sat in the chapel, quietly awaiting the forthcoming solo, wondering how many times the opening note would be hit before there was some sort of voice answering the response.

Taryn clenched her teeth as he turned his face toward the wall, childishly continuing to steadfastly ignore her musical introduction.

"Come on, Reed!" she whispered in a pleading tone. "Do it!"

"Yeah, Reed, do it!" a gruff male voice implored in a low, impatient tone from the other side of the curtain. "For heaven's sake let's get this show on the road, fella."

When the organ sounded again, it was with such belligerence that Reed was on his feet, and the mourners cringing in their seats, as the first note of "The Old Rugged Cross" rang out loud and clear in a male voice.

The rich, deep baritone made the wait more than worthwhile as he sang the old familiar song with sweet, honest simplicity. No one could possibly guess that what he was doing wasn't a natural thing for him and that he hadn't sung at funerals all his life. On the contrary, one would have sworn the good Lord had sent one of his messengers today, straight from a heavenly choir in honor of good, kind Martha Feagan.

Only Taryn saw the fear in his beautiful gray eyes as he sang verse after verse, his voice bringing comfort to the bereaved, hope to the weary, and compassion to those who had suffered the loss of an old friend. When the last note was played, Reed slumped down on the bench next to Taryn, perspiration dripping down his face.

The intoning voice of the minister filled the small chapel now as Taryn reached over and cradled him in her arms, waiting for the tension to seep slowly out of his body. "It was beautiful," she whispered lovingly in his ear.

"That was the hardest thing I've ever done in my life," he admitted in a ragged voice. "I sure hope Martha was listening."

"I'm sure she was," Taryn comforted as she patted him on the back in tender reassurance. That *was* a dirty thing to pull on anyone, but the situation warranted drastic measures! Biting pensively at her lip, she continued to pat his back absently as she tried to come up with some tactful way to break the news to him; he was going to have to drive the hearse to the cemetery, since the injuries to Foster and his wife during the storm had been more serious than first believed. Taryn had found out about this latest development only moments before the musical crisis. After racking her brain to come up with a quick solution, she had decided to call on her grandfather's neighbor Ferris to come to her aid. Ferris would drive the family car, Reed would drive the hearse, and she would drive the flower car. It was the only thing she could come up with on such short notice.

"May I speak with you outside for a moment, please?" she whispered in a pleasant voice.

Reed looked up, his eyes mirroring relief that he wasn't going to have to sit through the services. "Sure, let's get out of here."

The sound of distant, rolling thunder could be heard as they slipped out into the dim foyer together. "Oh, no," Taryn muttered, glancing out the window in despair. "It looks like it's going to rain again."

"It's probably just a light summer shower," Reed predicted, casting a quick glimpse toward the threatening clouds playing tag with each other across the darkening sky. "Well"—he gave a wide yawn and stretched his arms above his head, trying to ease some of the remaining tension out of his tired shoulders—"guess I'll cut out and go see about my Bronco."

Taryn watched the play of his muscles against his broad chest and wondered fleetingly for a minute what he would look like with his shirt off . . . and maybe his slacks. . . .

110

"Hey, I wish you wouldn't look at me that way," he protested gently.

"What way?" She felt the color rising in her cheeks as she hastily averted her eyes from his.

"You know 'what way.'"

"I was just looking at you," she said defensively. "Why should that upset you?"

"Because it makes me start wishing for things that can't be," he argued impatiently.

Taryn shrugged. "Now who's reading things into a conversation . . . or an innocent look?"

"I'm going to be married Saturday, Taryn. That's a simple fact. Up until three days ago, I never dreamed I would ever question that, but the last two days—" His voice broke off in frustration. "Well, hell. The last couple of days have started me thinking, and I don't like it!"

"I'm afraid I can't help you. You have to decide how, and with whom, you'll spend your life, Reed. If it'll help any, I'll try not to look at you again until you leave," she promised sourly.

"That sounds fair. I'll try not to look at you either." He grinned guiltily, his eyes lazily surveying her delectable derriere. "Or touch," he tacked on longingly.

The sound of the minister's closing remarks filtered from beneath the chapel door, turning Taryn's attention away from Reed's suggestive teasing as she focused her thoughts back on the hour. "It sounds like the services are over."

111

"Yeah. I guess I'll be running along. Better check on old Malcolm sometime this afternoon," he warned. "He's down on himself again today and he's still not eating like he should."

"Uh . . . Reed . . ." She had to break the bad news to him before he got away.

He turned at the front door he was about to open and met her sheepish countenance. "Yes?"

The mourners in the chapel heard a loud, muffled *"Oh no!"* as the final prayer was issued and they filed quietly past the casket to pay their final respects to Martha Feagan.

Fifteen minutes later a huffy Reed was helping Taryn load the floral tributes into the car. "Now, you remember. The bargain is you are to personally see that the tree is cut off my car today!" he reminded her as she stuck a huge bouquet of yellow mums in his arms. He sneezed violently, then pitched them into the back of the van.

"I will, I promise," she pacified, scooping up another wreath and handing it to him. She planned on keeping her promise. After his car was freed, *then* she would think of some other way to keep him around until he could see the frivolity of entering into a marriage with someone he didn't really love! She had suddenly formed the intense, indisputable opinion it was her Christian duty to save him from the jaws of marital disaster.

"Reverend Parsons, would you like to ride in the hearse?" Taryn invited as the minister made his way

112

out of the side door. The long black limousine was sitting under the canopy, being loaded by six older men to go to the cemetery, as the rain continued to fall.

"Oh, thank you, but no. I have my own car," he called back pleasantly.

"You're sure?" The ministers usually chose to ride to the cemetery and back with the funeral director.

"No, I'll just take my own car," he refused again firmly.

"If he wants to take his own car, let him take his own car," Reed said irritably, then sneezed loudly again. "Get off the poor man's back!"

"I was only thinking of you," she pointed out. "I thought it might make it easier if you had someone to keep you company on the drive to the cemetery." What she really meant was, someone to take his mind off the cargo he was carrying, but she discreetly refrained from saying so.

Reed paused in his loading and glared at her. "You mean it's just going to be me and ol' Martha again?"

"She won't cause you any more trouble, I'll personally guarantee it. Here, take this and blow your nose!" Taryn handed him a clean handkerchief and loaded the last bouquet of flowers into the van herself. Slamming the doors closed, she dusted off her hands and anxiously surveyed the line of cars beginning to form behind the long black car. "Oh, darn. I was hoping the rain would let up before we had to start, but it looks like it's set in for the day."

"Let's just go and get it over with," Reed grumbled just as another sneeze shattered his words.

"Just keep on the main road," Taryn instructed as she hopped into the van and turned the ignition. "The cemetery's about five miles from here on the right. You can't miss it."

Reed was still sneezing as he walked to the front of the hearse and got in, casting a suspicious eye in the back of the limousine. He wanted to be sure *every-thing* was closed up tight!

The funeral procession pulled slowly out of the drive, following the hearse, flower car, and family car. The rain seemed to be growing heavier as the cars solemnly wove their way toward the cemetery. The procession had almost reached its ultimate goal when the minister's car lurched forward a couple of times, then stalled. The cars in the line came to a halt as Taryn rolled down her window and tried to see what the problem was. From her vantage point she could hear the minister trying to restart his car without success. Reed jumped out of the hearse and walked over to speak with the minister, both of them shaking their heads and talking rapidly. The funeral procession was beginning to tie up traffic and motorists started honking their horns as Taryn slid out of the front seat of the van and hurried over to the two men.

"What's the matter?" she asked, hurriedly brushing her wet hair out of her eyes. Her dress was soaked through already and the thin fabric was clinging provocatively to her feminine curves.

"The minister's car ran out of gas," Reed explained as his eyes distraughtly took in her revealing attire. He quickly took off his jacket and wrapped it around her shivering body.

"I'm sorry, Taryn, my gas gauge isn't working properly and I thought I still had half a tank," the Reverend Parsons apologized with a chagrined smile on his kindly features.

"It happens to the best of us," Taryn said, trying to relieve his embarrassment.

"We'll have to push the car out of the way," Reed yelled above the downpour.

Ferris got out of the family car to help the two men as they grunted and groaned and pushed on the heavy four-door sedan amid the persistent blare of irate motorists trying to get around the long line of cars. Never in her whole life had Taryn had such a horrible time trying to conduct one simple burial service!

In an effort to speed up the process, Taryn rushed over to lend her feeble muscle power to those of the men shoving on the Reverend's car.

"What are you doing?" Reed snapped as she fell in beside him and heaved with all her might. "Go get back in the van before you drown!"

"We have to get this car out of the way and the line moving again," she puffed, straining every muscle in her body. "There's going to be a riot in a few minutes if we don't!"

"We can handle it without your help!" he shouted. "Now get back in the car and for heaven's sake keep that jacket on! I don't want every man out here ogling you!"

Taryn's heart fairly sang as she dropped back and let the men work up enough speed to roll the stalled car over to the side of the road. Reed had sounded almost jealous! Everyone returned to their respective vehicles, the minister riding in the hearse with Reed this time, and they soon had the procession rolling along smoothly again. When the cars pulled into the cemetery, Taryn groaned out loud as she saw the muddy roads Reed was trying to force the hearse through. Holding her breath and crossing her fingers, she prayed Reed would be able to get the hearse up the small incline to where the green canopy was spread out over the open grave site.

The thought had no more left her mind when the back wheel of the limousine sank to the axle in a puddle of deep, black mire.

When Reed slammed out of the hearse this time, there was a murderous glint to his eye as he leaned down and grimly surveyed the embedded wheel. He was mumbling some sort of unintelligible garble as Taryn shuffled, disheartened, over to the car and slumped against the fender in disgust.

"Well, this is a fine how-do-you-do," she announced flatly.

116

When he turned his stormy features in her direction, she was immensely thankful she wasn't a mind reader!

"Go get Ferris and the minister again. We're going to have to try to shove it out, but I want to warn you, I think we've got about as much chance of doing it as a snowball has in hell."

Taryn went after the two rain-drenched men and the process of shoving began all over again. She got in the car and tried to assist their efforts by rocking the car back and forth, but only succeeded in spinning the wheels and throwing a wall of mud over the three men. Ferris and the Reverend Parsons took the small discomfort in stride, but Taryn was mortified at Reed's language in front of a minister!

"Go get the pallbearers and anyone else available. We're going to have to carry Martha up the hill," he announced in a tightly controlled voice as he calmly spit mud out of his mouth. The whites of his eyes were the only clean thing on him now.

Taryn hurried to gather the pallbearers. Not one of them seemed overly anxious to get out in the monsoon, but ten minutes later the entourage were staggering their way up the rain-slicked hillside as the occupants of the other cars scattered like buckshot toward the dry cover of the canopy.

Taryn winced painfully as Reed went down on his knees several times trying to regain firm footing in the wet grass. The other men were having the same traction problem as they made their way precariously up the hill, trying to balance the heavy casket between them.

When they finally reached the grave site, everyone in the crowd heaved an audible sigh of relief.

The minister withdrew his Bible from his soaked jacket and gingerly tried to separate the wet, muddy pages to begin his final message.

Reed walked over to stand next to Taryn, his hair plastered against his face like a wet, dripping mop. He sneezed twice as they both edged as far away from the flowers as they could. By now Taryn was close to a nervous breakdown from the chaos of the last thirty minutes. She knew the pandemonium that had occurred could not be attributed to lack of responsibility from the Lassiter Funeral Home, but it still broke her heart to think of how all the dignity and solemnity of the hour had been cruelly stripped from Martha's services. She could only hope Millicent would forgive her eventually. Tears of frustration sprang to her eyes as a strong arm reached out and drew her close to the comfort of his strong body. Reed held her tenderly as she laid her head on his shoulder in weariness and listened to the droning voice of the Reverend Parsons. It felt so right to be here, cuddled in his arms as the rain beat down soundly on the green canvas. His fingers gently massaged her shoulders as they bowed their heads together in silent prayer. Taryn knew it was wrong for her to long for Reed's touch, wrong even to dream about any permanent relationship with him, yet her heart told her it was so very right.

She opened her eyes at the close of the prayer and stiffened perceptibly in Reed's arms. He felt the change in her body and glanced questioningly over at her. Motioning with her eyes toward a woman who must have weighed somewhere in the vicinity of two hundred and fifty pounds, Taryn frowned worriedly. The woman was sobbing hysterically, her massive body swaying back and forth in an unsteady motion. Taryn knew to watch for just such signs, signs that told her the woman was becoming so emotional she was going to faint. It wasn't an unusual thing to occur at a grave site, but her grandfather usually took control in these situations.

"See that heavyset woman standing over there next to the flowers?" Taryn whispered to Reed.

"Is that *one* woman? I thought I was looking at twins," Reed returned in a conspiratorial whisper, meant to coax a small smile from her serious face.

"I'm afraid she's going to faint," Taryn cautioned quietly.

Reed's eyes shot nervously over to the woman and he stepped quickly away from Taryn, reaching out to offer the woman his hand for support. The next thing Taryn knew, the woman gave a loud swooning sigh and, in a wild flurry of thrashing arms and legs, collapsed on Reed, burying him under her sizable bulk among the mound of flowers piled high by the grave site. Taryn gasped out loud, nearly becoming hysterical as her eyes searched the mound of human flesh pulverizing his body in a sea of pink and red carnations. Only the violent fit of ah-choos, followed by a series of painful groans assured her he was still alive as the crowd of mourners broke apart and scurried over to dig frantically through the flowers and rescue Reed and the overwrought lady.

"Oh, my poor darling," Taryn crooned as she pushed a clump of gladiolus off his battered body and brushed frantically at a clump of dirt mashed onto his nose and forehead. "You have had a simply horrible day, haven't you?"

"I think you could be safe in assuming that," he moaned, staring up at her in a catatonic state.

"Oh, here, let me help you up." She helped him rise to his feet, supporting his limp frame against hers. "I'm going to take you home and get you out of those wet clothes and into a tub of hot water before you catch a cold on top of everything else," she babbled, leading his dazed form in the direction of the van.

"Is it over? Is Martha buried?" he asked, giving her a stupefied grin.

"Yes, darling, it's all over. I'll ask Ferris and a couple of other men to finish up here, because I think you've had all you can stand for a day. Maybe they can get the hearse out of the mud hole. But don't you worry about it one little bit! There's no way I'm going to ask you to do one more thing for me today, because it just wouldn't be fair. Can you ever forgive me? I should have never been so mean to you and made you do all these things against your will, but you have to realize I didn't have another soul I could ask, you know, with the storm and all, but I do appreciate everything you've done for me I really do."

"Thank you—"

"Oh, you're so welcome, darling." She paused and hugged his filthy neck, her affection and appreciation for him spilling over. "Now you just lean on me and I'll have you home before you know it and then I'll fix us something good to eat. What do you like? Pork chops? I have some nice pork chops I can fix and maybe some stuffing. Do you like stuffing better than mashed potatoes? Well, anyway, we can both relax now that Martha has been taken care of and we can talk. You know, I think we really need to talk about Elaine and Gary—"

"Taryn!" Reed paused and sagged against her weakly. "You're rattling again."

"Oh. I am?"

"You are."

"I'm sorry," she apologized in a remorseful little voice.

Leaning over to touch his mouth briefly to hers, he whispered in an unmistakably affectionate voice, "Take us home, Motormouth."

"I'd be happy to." She returned his kiss happily. "And, with a little luck, I just might get to keep you!"

CHAPTER SEVEN

"Squaaawk, Malcolm is a bad boy. Squaaawk, Malcolm is a bad boy!"

Malcolm swung back and forth on his perch in a high-strung manner as Reed stretched his aching body out on the bed in Martin Lassiter's bedroom later that evening. On arriving back at the funeral home, he had immediately headed for the bathroom and a hot shower. If he had to cite a day in his memory that defied all explanation, this would be *the* one.

He closed his eyes for a moment and the image of Taryn Oliver drifted enticingly before him. Now, that was strange, and just a little bit irritating to him. Why should her face pop up instead of Elaine's? True, he did have a terrible weakness for redheads and she *did* have a shape that made his eyes keep pole-vaulting over in her direction—and that cute little posterior of hers . . . His eyes flew open guiltily and he forced his mind to take another direction. Elaine was going to have his hide if he didn't get to Santa Fe in the next couple of days. It had taken her and her mother months to plan this wedding and all the prenuptial parties and events that were taking place now. Reed rolled over on his side and listened to the rising wind rattling the old house. Now why, after all these months of total indifference, was he suddenly beginning to feel the noose of marriage tightening around his throat and nearly strangling him? Premarital jitters. Everyone had them, he assured himself confidently. Elaine and his marriage would be a good one, no matter what that nerve-racking redhead said! No, he didn't love Elaine, at least not with that blinding, overpowering kind of love Taryn spoke about. But he did like her, a lot, and they would have a nice, sane life together. He chuckled softly as he quietly contemplated what his life would be if he were married to that sexy mortician he had spent the last couple of days fighting with. Desire sprang up hot and totally unexpected at the thought of Taryn and himself sharing a marriage bed. Forcing the unwilling thought out of his mind, he rolled over again and stared at the ceiling.

"Squaaawk, Malcolm wants a Fig Newton. Squaaawk, Malcolm wants a Fig Newton!" the bird demanded belligerently.

"Malcolm has six Fig Newtons lying in the bottom of his cage right now that he's not eating," Reed replied dryly. "Malcolm's going to have a boot down his throat if he doesn't shut up and let me go to sleep," he added in a no-nonsense tone.

"Squaaawk, Reed's a baaad boy, Reed's a baaad boy!"

Well, at least he's let up on himself for a while, Reed thought sleepily.

A soft knock on the door interrupted the argument. "It's open," Reed called, sitting up on the side of the bed.

"Hi." The smell of a sultry perfume filtered lightly into the room as Taryn stepped inside carrying a tube of medicated analgesic in her hand. "How's your shoulder?"

Reed's hand went up absently to his sore shoulder, having forgotten for the moment the pain he had suffered when the heavyset woman had fallen on him earlier. "It's not bad," he protested, forcing his eyes away from the sexy peignoir she was wearing. The sheer pink material wasn't that skimpy, but it still did nothing to ease his already uncomfortable state of enforced celibacy.

"I found some medicine to rub on it," she offered, strolling over to where he sat on the edge of the bed. "Want me to put some on for you?"

"No, I don't think it needs any," he hedged, edging slightly away from her. "It's doing okay."

"I thought you said it was really bothering you when we were having dinner," she pursued. She sat down on the side of the bed, her face growing amused as he scooted even farther across the bed— away from her. "What's the matter?"

"Nothing. Why?"

"Oh, no reason, I just thought I better warn you, though, if you scoot any farther away from me, you're going to land on the floor," she teased. "I thought I'm the one who's supposed to be doing the scooting. Are you afraid I'm going to attack you again?"

"No." He grinned weakly. "To be honest, I'm afraid I'm going to attack you!"

Taryn sighed softly, trying hard not to let his words mean anything, but it was so tempting. Sitting here next to him, listening to the wind howl outside the small window, lent a touch of intimacy to the room that was beginning to steal over her and make her long for more than could rightfully be hers.

"Why the big sigh?" he asked perceptively, forcing himself to look at his hands and ignore the way her beautiful hair fell loosely across her creamy shoulders.

"No reason. Are you sure you wouldn't like some of this rubbed on your shoulder?" she asked whimsically, becoming increasingly aware of the growing sexual tension that had suddenly sprung up between them.

The soft glow of the bedside lamp caught the strawberry highlights of her hair as she held the tube up for his inspection, and he felt his insides turn into one big, painful knot. In all the years he had known Elaine, she had never once made him feel like he did at this moment, all warm and mushy inside. . . . In that one brief moment, Reed suddenly began to seriously question his forthcoming marriage. He knew with swift, unexplainable clarity that he was destined to hold this woman in his arms and make love to her, and when he did, nothing in his life would ever be the same again. The sun would still rise and set, wars would rage on, the poor would go hungry, the lonely would still cry themselves to sleep at night, and the sound of a child's laughter would still touch the hearts and light the faces of all who heard; but for Reed Montgomery, life would change.

"Taryn . . ." Her gaze told him she was feeling all that he was, yet neither one spoke for a moment. Finally, Reed heaved a defeated sigh and whispered softly, "You know this is crazy. We've only known each other three days—three days! Things like this just don't happen in three days!"

There was no need to put into words what he was referring to. Taryn knew without a doubt because she had questioned the sanity of it herself. Her head nodded slowly in shame. She did know that. Here was a man who had walked into her life and turned it upside down in a scant three days, a man who belonged to someone else. But those things no longer held meaning when she looked into the deep silvery pools of his eyes and saw the longing that she herself could no longer deny.

"What are we going to do? I don't want to hurt Elaine," she whispered. And she meant it. She knew what they both were contemplating could cause great pain for all involved.

"I don't want to hurt her either," he confessed.

"What I'm feeling right now has nothing to do with her, yet the consequences will affect her."

"Maybe it's just a sexual attraction that will pass after it has been fulfilled," she suggested in a faltering voice. That was entirely possible. She had heard of such things, although she herself had never practiced the theory.

"I hadn't thought of it that way, but maybe you're right." His voice sounded somewhat relieved. "That's probably what it is." His hand moved out to hesitantly cover hers, his fingers gently massaging hers to tingling awareness. "I suppose we're doomed to find out one way or the other. . . ."

Her heart thudded painfully as he moved closer and his lips moved down to touch hers with silky softness. With a soft sigh, her arms moved up around his neck and she tilted her mouth upward to accept his kiss, which came without hesitation as he moaned softly and pulled her closer to him. His kiss was poignantly sweet, in no way demanding, only seeking to give and receive the pleasure they both knew was awaiting them. His mouth brushed hers with tantalizing slowness as he nibbled at the corners of her lips, quickly shattering the remains of any composure she might have had.

"You taste as good as you look," he murmured, trailing his mouth down the slender column of her neck. His touch was gentle and exploring, and she could tell he was keeping a tight leash on his passion. His hands sensuously touched her skin, drinking in the feel of her loveliness as his mouth found hers once more for a deep kiss. They lay back on the bed and her fingers found their way under his shirt. She longed to touch him, to discover all the mysteries she had only guessed at until now.

"You want me to take my shirt off," he murmured, stealing honeyed kisses from her willing mouth. "Or better yet, why don't you take it off for me?"

"Reed." Her body was responding to his caresses with a growing need that would soon be demanding complete fulfillment. She vaguely remembered there was one thing she had to do before she gave her love, her total being, to another man.

"What's the matter, sweetheart? Am I going too fast?" he whispered. "I know I probably am, but you can't possibly know how very much I've wanted to hold you like this. Ever since you came into my arms in the basement during the storm. Do you remember doing that . . . ? I was scared to death you would feel my need for you that day," he admitted, moving that need against her now in tantalizing persuasion of his words. "It's been there all along, Taryn, from the minute I laid eyes on you. At first it scared me. I've never felt this way about a woman, never felt the thrill or the joy of being with someone who makes me grow weak with longing when I just look at her." His voice was filled with soft wonder as he buried his hands in the thickness of her hair and inhaled its perfumed fragrance, murmuring her name tenderly.

"Reed, before we make love . . . there's something I have to do," she pleaded breathlessly, feeling her body spring achingly alive with all the feelings she had once thought were dead and gone forever.

"Now? Oh, I had forgotten about that." He assumed she would want to protect herself and he silently berated himself for not thinking of it first.

"Would you give me a few minutes alone, then come to my room?" She lovingly traced the outline of his masculine features as she gazed up into his passion-laden eyes. "There's something very important I must do."

"I'll be there in five minutes," he promised in a voice growing huskier with passion by the moment. They exchanged another long series of lingering kisses before he reluctantly rolled off her and let her go. Her knees felt like water as she made her way across the hall, her lips tingling from his passionate lovemaking.

When she entered her bedroom, she hurried over to the bed to pick up the small photograph that had been so much a part of her life the last year. She fingered the outline of her husband's face tenderly as tears gathered gently in her eyes. A tear dripped silently on the picture frame as she reached for a handkerchief and dabbed at her eyes. She dried her eyes and blew her nose soundly, then walked over and opened the bottom drawer of her dresser and started lovingly to place the photo beneath a pile of sweaters she had worn in high school. She whispered a prayer in a sheepish voice as she closed the drawer.

"Listen, God, I'm not so sure Reed feels as strongly about all this as I do so, if you aren't too busy up there and it wouldn't be a lot of trouble, I sure would appreciate your help the next few days. You know . . . make it possible for Elaine not to be hurt too badly by all this and make Reed realize he loves *me* and can't live without me. Thanks!" She leaned against the bureau and took a deep breath just as Reed knocked softly on her door.

"Come in." She hurried over to the doorway as he quietly entered the room.

"Everything all right?"

"For the first time in a very long time, everything is just fine," she assured him, taking his hand and gently leading him toward her bed. His arm came out to pull her up against him as his mouth eagerly enfolded hers. For a brief moment they held each other tightly, their mouths molding and plying hungrily. His mouth left hers after a while, moving down the curve of her face and finally settling at the base of her throat.

"Who were you talking to?" he murmured.

"Were you listening?" she scolded, shivering as his tongue traced along the swell of her breasts.

"No . . ." he replied meekly, "I had just started to knock on your door when I heard your voice. I didn't hear anything you said," he assured, "but I can't help being curious. . . ."

"I was praying and saying good-bye, darling." She

brought his face back up to cup gently between her hands.

"There will be no one sharing our bed when we make love, Reed. I promise you." Her eyes sweetly told him that her promise was sincere and straight from her heart.

Whatever differences they had quickly dissolved like cotton candy on the tongue as her arms pulled him into their loving shelter and he buried his face in the perfumed fragrance of her neck, whispering of his great, overpowering need of her. Taryn gently pushed him away and her fingers found the buttons on his shirt as she gazed warmly into his beautiful eyes. "I want to see every delicious part of you," she confessed, undoing the buttons in deliberate provocation. "You can think me shameful, but I don't care. I want to know what you feel like, look like, taste like. . . ." Her mouth followed her words as the first few buttons came loose.

"Oh, lady, I love your way of thinking," he groaned as she slipped the last button through the loop. The shirt came off, then the belt, his socks, his slacks, and then she was finally down to the delectable, mouth-watering icing on the cake.

"To think, I thought you might be *shy* about this," he said as he grinned in a silly, smug, completely chauvinistic way.

She showed him just how totally wrong he could be, shattering that infuriating confidence of his to smithereens as she rid him of the last vestige preventing her ultimate pleasure. Her eyes darkened passionately as she surveyed the wondrous treasure she had discovered. A light coating of golden brown hair covered his athletic physique and he was built exactly as she had imagined he would be. The soft smattering of hair weaved its way across his broad chest, down his arms, and along the length of his powerful thighs. Taryn knew without a doubt she was going to overindulge on "dessert" tonight as her mouth nibbled smoothly along his broad shoulder muscle. Tonight would be a special time in their lives and she longed to make it as memorable for Reed as it would be for her.

Reed moaned as her mouth became more aggressive, and his hands slipped the filmy pink robe from her shoulders and let it float gently to the floor. Seconds later her gown joined the sheer fabric and he gathered her satiny body up to nest provocatively between his taut thighs.

"You're making me crazy, do you know that?" he murmured, letting her feel his awesome need for her, as his hands began slowly to acquaint themselves with her gentle swelling curves.

Their kisses turned hot and hungry now as he laid her on the bed and his hands moved eagerly over her, exploring every bit of unfamiliar terrain. Kissing her breasts to soft, budding fullness, he suddenly seemed to have lost all previous control of his emotions as he moved to claim her, filling her with his elemental power, blocking out all rational thought as

132

they soared together in a world of ecstasy that was so beautiful, so awesome, it took their breath away. The joy they were bringing each other sang through their veins as she met his ardor with her own until the world dissolved into a million tiny stars for them, casting them out into a heavenly void.

Taryn buried her face in his broad chest, placing heated kisses on his warm, moist skin, her hands tenderly guiding him back to the real world as he slumped against her, still murmuring her name.

Only the sound of the wind could be heard as they lay locked in each other's arms, lovingly exchanging sweet, languorous kisses.

"You don't happen to have any ketchup with you, do you?" Reed murmured in a shaken voice.

"Ketchup? Are you serious? What do you want with ketchup at a time like this?" she asked incredulously.

"Well, I think I'm just about ready to eat my words," Reed admitted shyly.

Taryn leaned on her elbow and playfully kissed the tip of his nose. "You mean those famous last words about not having ever experienced that formidable, devastating power of love? *Those* words?"

Reed's eyes grew clouded as he rolled on his back and stared thoughtfully up at the ceiling. "Love? I'm still not sure about that, Taryn. Love is such a . . . 'forever after' word."

"And you're not ready to accept that kind of love," she finished in a small, troubled voice.

"Does that bother you?"

"Not really. I think everyone has to reach a point in their lives when they're willing to let go of their love and place it in someone else's hands. That isn't an easy thing to do. In fact, it's very scary. But, Reed, you—are—willing to place your life in Elaine's hands, so why does the thought of placing it in my hands scare you?"

"I'm willing to place my life in her hands, Taryn, not my love. There's a big difference."

"That sounds very cold and callous, Reed, and I happen to know you're not that way at all."

"Maybe I am, Taryn. All my adult life I've had to think of someone else's wants and needs and I'm just darn tired of having other people chart my destiny. For once in my life I'd like to be able to make my own decisions. Can you understand that?" His voice sounded accusing, almost as if he were blaming her for the unsavory predicament he now found himself in.

"Well, don't blame me, Reed. I'm not the one making you marry a woman you don't love just so you can have a topnotch position in her daddy's law firm," she reminded him curtly.

Her angry words took him by surprise. "That's a rotten thing to say!"

"Rotten, but true. You said yourself you were marrying Elaine for the position in her father's company."

"I'm not marrying her solely for that reason," he

protested. "Elaine and I have a lot of things in common. We've known each other for years. We like the same movies, the same type food, we have the same taste in music—"

"And, I suppose, her parents have to haul their money to the bank in a dump truck," she interjected curtly.

"They're not hurting, if that's what you're getting at, but that has nothing whatsoever to do with my decision," he told her tensely. "I have always made my own way in the world and I always will!"

"Are you sleeping with her?" Taryn knew his answer was only going to bring her pain, but she asked him anyway.

Reed reached over and pulled her onto his chest, kissing her into silence. When they parted a long time later, he chose to answer her question the kindest way he knew possible. "If I were sleeping with her, I'd never tell you or anyone else. That happens to be a very personal thing between a man and woman, don't you agree?"

"You are! I knew it," she accused him.

"Now, look! What about Gary? The idea that you loved another guy enough to marry him doesn't exactly thrill me either!"

"That doesn't count," she justified meekly. "That was before I ever knew you existed. What I felt for Gary is so much different from what I'm feeling for you, Reed. There's no comparison, actually. Gary and I met and had a whirlwind romance. We were married a short three weeks after we met and he died six weeks after the marriage. Sometimes I look back on that time of my life and think that it was all a dream. What we shared was quick and explosive and wonderful, but sometimes . . . sometimes I have to think really hard to remember what he kissed like, or how he smelled, or even what color his eyes were or how his voice sounded. I was so crushed and bitter over his death and I wanted so desperately to hang on to what we had, but lately . . . ?" She paused and absently ran her hands through the hair on Reed's chest. "I've been so darn lonely."

"It sounds to me like you were deeply in love with him," Reed murmured.

"I was. In a wild, crazy, totally unexplainable way, because that was the kind of guy he was, wild, crazy, and completely unexplainable. There have been times in the last year that I've wondered if our attraction for each other would have lasted. Gary was a natural and free spirit. I like things more steady and down-to-earth. Who knows, after the shine wore off our marriage, we may have woken up one day to find out we really didn't have anything at all."

Reed's eyes searched her face and found her words to be genuine and honest. "And you think we could have something more lasting . . . the 'forever after' kind people are always talking about?"

"I think it wouldn't hurt to explore that possibility," she admitted, tracing the outline of his lips with the tip of her long, perfectly shaped nail.

"The thought doesn't scare you?"

"What? 'Forever after' love?" She laughed. "I deal in the 'forever after' every day of my life," she teased him.

He gave an exaggerated groan as he nipped at her finger with his strong white teeth. "Now, there's another problem we haven't discussed. Your nerve-racking occupation."

"What about it?"

"Taryn, honey, even if we didn't have all these other obstacles standing in the way of our relationship, there is *no* way on earth that I could live in a funeral home on a day-to-day basis. These last few days have me walking around wishing for an extra set of eyes in the back of my head, and if I had to live through one more day like today . . ."

"Silly!" She stopped his flow of words with persuasive kisses. "Let's not even think about that problem until we're able to solve some of the larger ones.

"Reed?" she asked a few minutes later. "Do you realize, until a few minutes ago we actually didn't know anything about each other? I don't even know where you live!"

Reed sat up and propped the pillow on the headboard and reached for a cigarette out of his shirt pocket and lit it. Drawing Taryn back into the shelter of his arm, he began to fill in the empty pages of his life for her. "That's simple enough to clear up. I've lived in Kansas City since I graduated from law school. Elaine . . ." He paused and drew her closer as he felt her stiffen again at the mention of his fiancée's name. "Elaine and I have worked in the same law office for the last couple of years. When her dad found out about our engagement, he offered both of us a position in his firm. Since it didn't make any difference to me where we lived, I let Elaine make the decision. Naturally, she chose to go home. She wanted to have the wedding in Santa Fe anyway since her grandparents' health prevented them from making the trip to Kansas City, so she left for home a couple of months ago to plan the wedding and look for an apartment while I stayed behind and cleared up last-minute business. As you already know, I was headed to Santa Fe when the storm caught me."

Taryn had never felt so miserable as she listened to his somber words. "I wish I hadn't asked. It makes the wedding and Elaine seem so real now," she managed to say beyond the tight lump in her throat.

"They *are* real," he replied solemnly, absently stroking her hair. "I want you to know I don't make a habit of this sort of thing, Taryn, this is the first time I've been with another woman since I became seriously involved with Elaine."

"I'm sorry. I feel so cheap." She buried her head in his shoulder and fought with her warring feelings. Tonight would only be a brief, sweet remembrance. She now realized it was just too late in Reed's life to change his plans.

"Cheap! Don't you ever let me hear you say that again," he demanded in an astonished tone. "What happened tonight was not a cheap, tawdry roll in the hay, Taryn, and I won't have you dirtying it up with those kinds of thoughts."

"What happened was wrong, Reed, and I'm afraid I instigated it to the fullest. I seriously thought you didn't love Elaine and I could save you from making what I consider the mistake of your life. Not only for you but for Elaine, too. But I see now that it doesn't matter. You have to do what you have to do."

"I'm confused," he confessed. "I have no idea which way to turn or what to do next."

Taryn knew she shouldn't do it, but her arms automatically tightened around his neck and she began slowly to kiss away the look of pain that now clouded his face.

He reached over and put out his cigarette, then drew her back into his arms. "You're one lovely lady and I'll never forget this night," he promised, capturing her mouth with almost savage intensity this time.

Their kisses turned fiery once more as their passion returned in full force. Reed had just kissed his way down to Taryn's navel, all thoughts of right and wrong put aside for the time being, when the phone rang in the other room.

"Let it ring," he urged, taking her breath away with a demanding kiss that caused her insides to quiver.

"I can't," she moaned. "It might be business."

"Business? This time of night?"

"We're on call twenty-four hours a day. You stay

right here and don't you dare go away," she warned, reaching for her housecoat. "I mean it, don't move!" It might be wrong, but they could only be hung for their crime once!

"I'm lying here nude in a house that's old and creaking, with a downstairs that is a funeral parlor, and the pretty redheaded mortician I'm in the process of making mad, passionate love to is creeping around in her nightgown answering telephones that're going to lead to God only knows what this time, and you honestly feel it's necessary to tell me not to go anywhere? Don't worry. I'll be here," he promised her dryly.

"Make sure you do." She stole one final kiss filled with enough promise to keep a man in bed for the next six months if asked, then rushed to answer the persistently ringing phone.

CHAPTER EIGHT

"Boo!" Taryn sneaked up behind the man standing in front of the kitchen sink rinsing off a head of lettuce, and poked him playfully in the ribs.

Reed let out a nervous yelp and jumped two feet off the floor as a head of lettuce flew straight up in the air then dropped to the ground and landed at his bare feet.

"Will you cut that out!" he demanded impatiently, leaning over to pick the head back up and toss it in the sink.

Taryn giggled and wrapped her arms around his waist. "I'm sorry, did I frighten you?"

"You little witch, you know you scared the pants off me creeping around yelling boo!" Reed turned around to face her and drew her back to him for a long, welcoming kiss, his actions belying his grumpy words.

"You were supposed to stay right where you were," she reminded him, kissing his eyes and nose and face. "I went back to bed and you were gone."

"I got hungry," he complained with a grin.

"What in the world are you wearing?" She stood back and surveyed his attire, laughter welling up in her. He was wearing her old blue chenille housecoat, and although it was big on her, it couldn't come close to fitting his broad, muscular frame. The front of the robe gaped open shamefully as he turned around and around, preening for her like a conceited peacock. "How do you like it? Turn you on?"

"Where are your pants?" she asked in mock despair, enjoying every minute of his risqué performance.

"I just told you. You scared them off me." He shrugged innocently, pulling her back in his arms for another hungry kiss.

"Why are you wearing *my* housecoat, you idiot?"

"I didn't want to get dressed, since I knew we'd be going back to bed, so I put the robe on to come out here and fix a sandwich. Now that you're back, I seem to have lost my appetite . . . for food, that is." He affectionately nuzzled her neck, drawing her into the confines of the robe with him. "What took you so long? I missed you."

"Oh, the call was from the clinic."

"Everything all right?"

"Yes, it wasn't concerning Grandpa. It was . . . business." She caught her breath as his tongue licked sensuously at her ear, poking playfully in and out, sending shivers racing down her spine.

"Don't you think we should mosey on back upstairs and get back to what we were doing before the phone interrupted us?" he whispered in a low, suggestive voice. His hands had found what they were seeking and she was beginning to be caught up in a new web of growing arousal. "I can skip my sandwich," he coaxed her with a series of persuasive kisses.

"We can't. I have to leave," she confided in a regretful voice.

"Leave?" He pulled back a fraction and curiously searched her face. "For where?"

"The clinic."

"I thought you said everything was all right with your grandfather."

"It is, silly," she assured, kissing him one final time before she reluctantly stepped out of his embrace. "I told you. I have to go there on . . . business."

Enlightenment slowly crept over his puzzled countenance as his arms dropped back to his sides in disappointment. "Oh. *That* kind of business."

"Yes, *that* kind of business. I don't suppose you'd consider going with me again?" She grimaced, and braced herself for the explosion that would surely follow.

Heaving a tired sigh, he ran his fingers through his hair and silently pondered the question for a moment. Finally he asked in a reluctant voice, "What would I have to do this time?"

"Nothing, really. Just help me lift . . . something on a stretcher," she hedged.

He walked back to the sink and tore off a chunk of

lettuce, chewing thoughtfully on it as he carefully mulled her request over in his mind. "I suppose you'll have to go by yourself if I don't?"

"That's right. I can manage if you don't think you feel up to it, though," she added quickly. After all, he had done more for her today than even Gary would have done, she reminded herself.

He leaned against the sink and crossed his arms, bringing a lopsided grin to Taryn's face once more as she surveyed his disreputable attire showing off every ounce of his impressive masculine traits.

"What are you laughing about now, Redhead?"

"You and your ridiculous housecoat."

His grin took a definite turn to wicked as he noticed the path her eyes were taking. "Am I becoming nothing but a common, ordinary sex object to you already?"

She tilted her head and soberly contemplated what he so smugly felt assured had brought her to that captive state. "Ummm . . . sex object maybe, but common, ordinary . . . naw, even with my limited experience, I don't think so." Her grin was as wicked as his now.

"Come here, Ms. Oliver," he ordered softly as his eyes darkened in renewed passion.

"I don't think I should." She slowly backed away from him, her smile growing broader. "Something tells me you are going to try to delay my call to work."

"Don't try to play games and run from me. I'll

144

come after you," he challenged, still using that low, sexy voice.

"Not necessarily. It depends in what direction I run," she countered. "Now, should I choose to run toward the front parlor, I'd probably be more than safe. . . ."

He took a step forward and caught her back into his arms, pulling her down on the kitchen chair with him.

"Let go! I don't have anything on under my robe," she protested, feeling the warmth and firmness of his masculinity meet her bare bottom.

"What a shame," he said in a voice that didn't have one shred of regret in it.

For the next five minutes they kissed and touched and murmured in happy, contented sighs. It was Reed's turn to pull away this time as he groaned and stood up, scooping her up in his arms, whispering against her mouth, "Let's take a quick bath, then get started on your business, so we can get back to *our* business."

"You're going with me!" she squealed in delight. "Oh, thank you!" Her arms clasped tightly around his neck, and as they walked up the stairs they kissed heatedly. She knew his going with her to the clinic was a tremendous concession for Reed to make, and her love for him grew by leaps and bounds.

Walking into the hall bathroom, he turned on the bathtub faucets with his mouth still welded to hers. Their robes were quickly discarded and they spent the next few minutes playfully washing each other, pausing only long enough to steal long, languid kisses.

"You know what you're doing to me, don't you?" he murmured in a husky tone as they slid down in the warm water and let it surround them completely. He shifted to pull her wet body on top of his, moving intimately against her.

"No, what?" she asked innocently, her teeth playfully biting his shoulder. She knew the effect she was having on him and silently reveled in her power.

"You're forcing me to do something I don't think I should do . . . at least not right now," he argued in a practical voice.

"I'm not doing anything," she denied innocently, nibbling on his earlobe and moving in rhythm with his swaying body.

"Then you want me to go ahead and do it?" he prodded, fully aware of her intent to torment him.

"That's up to you," she returned primly, running the tip of her tongue around the outline of his bottom lip. He surged against her and they kissed for a few moments. "You're going to have to make up your mind," she encouraged as their lips finally parted. "It's growing very late . . . we really should be going."

"Well, if you're sure . . ." He reached down and pulled out the stopper, letting the soothing water drain away. Still passionately kissing her, he waited until the tub was empty, then replaced the plug and turned the cold water on full blast. Her eyes widened as she realized what he had done, and she screamed as the malicious rush of cold water seeped up around their bodies.

"What are you doing!" she screeched.

"Cooling us down so we can go to work," he returned in a totally innocent voice. "What did you think I meant?"

"Ohhh . . . you idiot!" She slapped him across the face with her wet washcloth and exited the tub in a fit of temper. He was right behind her, laughing deviously as he scooped her up in a towel and briskly rubbed her dry. Before he was through, her anger was long forgotten and they were trading passionate kisses once more.

"You sure do have a lot of freckles," he commented, surveying her rosy pink body as he handed the towel to her and motioned for her to return the favor.

"I know." She began to rub his back briskly. "At the slightest hint of sun they pop out like dandelions!"

His hand reached out and stilled her flying hands, his face turning serious for the first time as he looked into her eyes.

Her smile grew tender as she lovingly ran her fingers through the wet, dark waves of his hair. "What is it? Why are you looking at me like that?" she prompted softly.

"I'd like to see you when those freckles fade," he stated simply, "in the winter and in the fall. . . ."

Her hazel eyes dropped bashfully away from his silvery gray ones. "Isn't this something? You know, I've never done anything this crazy and wild in my whole life," she confessed.

Tipping her face gently back up to meet his, he smiled. "I know. And, if it helps any, I haven't either."

"What do you think? You think we both have gone completely out of our gourds?" she asked with a perky tilt of her head.

"That's very possible." He nodded. "In fact, that thought has entered my mind more than once in the last three days."

Another lingering kiss was shared before they finally parted to get dressed. When Reed came downstairs fifteen minutes later, Taryn was waiting for him. He looked so breathtakingly handsome in a pair of light blue dress jeans with a dark blue shirt tucked neatly in the waistband that it took all the willpower she could muster not to run over and throw herself in his arms.

While she was dressing, she had come to the conclusion that she was going to have to start restraining herself around him. Their impetuous actions were only going to make it harder on both of them when the time came for him to leave. And, she knew without a doubt, that time would come.

Reed walked over to the chair where she was sitting and leaned down and kissed her. "You look cute. I've never seen you in jeans before."

"Thanks. You look cute too. Much better than that horrible bathrobe you were wearing earlier," she teased, carefully avoiding his gaze.

"You think so?"

"I think so."

Stealing another quick kiss, he took her hand and pulled her to her feet. "Well, we might as well go and get your new . . . customer." With one arm draped casually around her waist, he walked with her through the kitchen and out the back door. The night air was warm and balmy as they strolled out to the four-car garage and opened the door.

"I suppose we're taking the hearse," he said, frowning.

"No, we can take the van if you'd rather."

"That's up to you, honey." He called her "honey" with such ease, it was as if they had known each other all their lives.

"The hearse," she decided, knowing that it would be more practical.

"I'll drive," he announced, holding out his hand for the keys. Gratefully handing them to him, she hurried around and got in on the passenger side.

The car roared to life and Reed backed it smoothly out of the drive. Seconds later they were driving down the main road leading to the clinic.

"You remembered! I didn't think you would," she

149

complimented, surprised he had recalled the way without having to have his memory refreshed.

"Oh, I'm truly amazing," he admitted with a sexy wink. "Haven't you noticed that yet? Hey! What are you doing way over there?" He reached over and pulled her close to his side. "This is where gorgeous redheads belong."

Taryn had to agree it was as his arm came around her, and she snuggled her head on his shoulder in contentment. This was not very ethical, she had to admit, but it was certainly very nice.

The clinic came in view too quickly to suit either one of them. Reed parked the limousine according to Taryn's instructions beside a side door leading into the clinic. Reaching into the back, he helped her withdraw a cot and wheel it in the doorway.

"The patient's name is Ralph Morliss," Taryn mused, referring to the slip of paper she held in her hand.

They wheeled the cot down the dimly lit hallway. "Why don't you take the stretcher into room two eighteen and get Mr. Morliss ready while I stop at the nurses' desk and let them know we're here."

"Now, look!" The cot came to a screeching halt. "Don't push your luck, Redhead. Consider yourself darn lucky I even consented to come, let alone send me in one of those rooms by myself!"

"Oh, all right," she said. "Wait here and I'll be back as soon as I get things squared away." She walked off down the hall in the direction of the nursing desk, leaving Reed leaning indolently against the wall.

Five minutes later he realized that he was starving. His earlier thoughts of a sandwich had been aborted in favor of more appealing things, but now his stomach told him it needed food—fast! Glancing down the hallway, he saw a nurse emerge from a small room down the corridor carrying a soft drink and a candy bar. Digging in his jeans pocket for some loose change, he walked down the hall and bought a package of corn chips and a can of soda pop and walked back to where the cot was standing. The snack did nothing to appease his appetite, and when Taryn failed to appear ten minutes later, he returned to the small room and bought two more candy bars and another bag of corn chips.

She had been gone for over twenty minutes when he started to grow impatient. *The smell of the hospital is beginning to make me sick,* he thought, forgetting to take into account the two bags of corn chips, two candy bars, and the can of soda pop he had just devoured.

Summoning up the nerve to get started on the task of transporting Ralph Morliss to the waiting cot, he wheeled the stretcher up to the nurses' desk and brought it to an abrupt halt. The nurse on duty glanced up expectantly.

"What room is Morliss in?" he mumbled. He couldn't remember what room number Taryn had mentioned earlier.

The nurse's eyes lit up appreciatively at the handsome man peering skittishly over the desk at her. "Why, hello," she purred. "May I help you?"

"Hello. What room is Morliss in?" he repeated, his fingers anxiously twisting the edge of the white sheet lying on the cot.

The nurse stood up and came around to look up at the tall, good-looking stranger. She had been a nurse for fifteen years in this clinic and she had never seen anything this magnificent standing in front of her desk before. "I'm sorry, what patient did you want to see?" she asked again, stalling for more time to make his acquaintance.

Reed had not failed to miss the female-predator gleam in her eye and it made him more nervous than he already was. Where in the devil had Taryn disappeared to!

"What's your name, handsome?" The nurse smiled a sultry silent invitation.

She might be looking for a good time, but he wasn't. At least, not with her! He didn't like blondes *or* nurses! Losing all patience with the situation he found himself in, he barked out his request once more. "Morliss! What room's Morliss in, lady!"

Flinching at his gruff demeanor, the nurse snapped up a chart, her eyes hurriedly scanning the list, seething quietly under her breath. *He may be cute, but he sure has a nasty disposition!* "Morris is in room two twenty!" she snapped.

"Thank you!" Wheeling his cart around in a

haughty manner, he resisted the urge to thumb his nose at the pushy nurse as he streaked back down the hallway, pushing the cot at a dead run. One of its wheels had begun to wobble unevenly, making a loud clacking noise as he worked his way down the quiet hallway, trying to read the door numbers in the dim lighting. The cot slowed, then rolled to a halt in front of room 220.

Hordes of nervous butterflies rose up in his stomach as he thought about what awaited him beyond the closed door. Taking a deep breath, he cautiously pushed the door open and groaned softly when he saw the room was pitch-black and that Taryn was nowhere to be seen.

He shrugged, deciding his task might be easier if he didn't have to look at what he was putting on the cart. He carefully wedged the cot through the doorway and then tiptoed over to the bed. He stood on his toes and tried to peek at the figure lying on the bed through the faint ray of light shining from the window. His heart sank. This one was another big one. *Well, Montgomery, you're not going to get the job done by standing around dreading it,* he chided himself. *Let's get this thing over with.*

He brought the cot to the side of the bed. Reed stood for a moment assessing the still form sprawled on the bed, trying to figure out the best way to go about this. He shook his head in disbelief. How had he ever gotten himself in this mess to begin with? If it wasn't for the fact he had fallen head over heels in

153

love with that redhead . . . His thoughts came to a sudden halt. In love with the redhead? Was he in love with the redhead?

The fact hit him hard and fast. He *was* in love with Taryn Oliver! He shook his head again as if to clear out the stunning thought. When had *that* happened and what was he going to do about it? Great balls of fire! He had only known her three days . . . three miserable days! Maybe his feelings for her were a direct result of his new surroundings. No, that's not it, he thought miserably, he *was* in love with her, plain and simple, but was it too late to do anything about it? Putting the disturbing puzzle aside for the time being, he went back to his immediate dilemma: how to get Mr. Morliss on the cot without touching him. Reed wasn't sure it could be done, but he *was* sure he was going to try everything within his power to accomplish that feat.

Stifling a sneeze, he pulled the ends of the bottom sheet out, then pulled the top sheet over the entire body, creating a makeshift sling. *You would think someone had already done all this!* he grunted, silently bemoaning the fact that it was impossible to get good help anymore!

Now he had a nice neat bundle. The only problem was how to switch it over to the cart. Ralph was pretty hefty, so Reed was going to have all he could do to make the switch alone. Climbing up on the bed, he braced one leg on the rail and started to ease the sheet slowly toward the cart. He paused for a moment. Had Morliss moved? A cold sweat beaded across his forehead as he sat perfectly still for a moment, barely breathing. No. It was only his overactive imagination. Taking another deep breath, he tugged at the sheet again, this time managing to move the body an inch or two in the right direction. Where in the *hell* was Taryn! He wiped at the perspiration dripping down his neck now. He should have waited, he decided. He just wasn't cut out for this sort of thing. Well, it was too late to back out now. A couple more good heaves should see the job finished, then he could get out of here. He sneezed once more, nearly knocking over a bouquet of flowers sitting on the nightstand next to the bed. Why, dear Lord, if I had to fall in love, did it have to be with a mortician?

Straddling the broad bundle now, Reed grunted and shoved once more just as "Morliss" sat straight up and let out an ear-piercing scream.

"What is going on? *Help! Mugger! Pervert!*" the bundle shouted at the top of its lungs in a high feminine screech.

Reed was so stunned, his first instinct was to pass out cold. Instead, his basic instincts took over and he slapped his hand over the screaming woman's mouth, trying to still the angry shrieks of hysteria.

"Quiet down! I'm not a pervert, lady. I'm from the funeral home!" he shouted above her screaming voice.

The screams turned from frightened to horrified now as the woman grabbed a pillow and began battering him around his shoulders, as if he were a punching bag.

"Funeral home! *Help! Somebody please help me!*" she roared at the top of her lungs.

The two rolled off the bed in a tumble of sheets, flogging arms and pillows amid loud screams and bellows of pain as the woman soundly thrashed Reed's cowering body, repeating over and over in a shrill, authoritative voice that *she* wasn't ready for a mortician yet!

The door flew open and the room flooded with light as two nurses ran in and began to separate the dueling duo.

"Mrs. Morris! Mrs. Morris, please calm down!" One of the nurses grabbed the pillow out of the over-wrought woman's hands, but not before she could prevent her from getting in one more sound whack, knocking Reed flat on his back as he struggled to get up.

"He's from the funeral home!" Mrs. Morris protested, starting after him again. "He was trying to get me on that horrible . . . cart!"

It took both nurses to protect Reed this time as he staggered dazedly to his feet.

"It was a mistake, lady! Just a simple mistake!" he groaned weakly, cowering behind one of the nurses.

From out of nowhere Taryn suddenly appeared in the doorway, her face growing distressed as she quickly assessed the situation. "Oh, Reed, what's going on!"

Reed was by her side, clinging to the hem of her jacket, much as a small child would, as he incoherently tried to babble his side of the story. By now the hallway had begun to fill with people, all of them craning their necks to see what the commotion was about.

The nurses were trying to work Mrs. Morris's considerable bulk back on the bed as the woman bellowed hysterically that all she had was minor surgery and she couldn't be in need of a mortician yet!

"I was only trying to help," Reed protested in a numb state as Taryn gently led him out of the room. "How was I to know I was in the wrong room? I thought I would surprise you and have Ralph Morliss all loaded and ready to go. So I went to the desk and asked the nurse, 'What room's Morliss in?' and she batted her fake eyelashes at me and said 'What's your name, handsome' and I sure wasn't in any mood for a flirty, blond-headed nurse, so I said, 'Morliss, what room is Morliss in,' and she said, 'Room two twenty.' I swear to you, Taryn, she said room *two twenty,* so I went down there and started to load . . . that thing on the cot and all of a sudden this crazy person was screaming and batting me over the head with her pillow shouting, *'Help! Mugger! Pervert!'* and I kept trying to tell her I wasn't there to rob her *or* to attack her, for cripes sake! But she kept screaming and banging me over the head with her pillow." He paused and rubbed his head in bewilderment. "My stomach hurts. Do you have any Pepto-Bismol with you?"

Taryn stopped and put her arms around him and gave him a reassuring hug. "Do you realize you're rattling on just like I do?"

"Oh, no! You have me doing it too? I want to go home, Taryn," he pleaded in a voice like a frightened child's.

"I know, darling, I'll take you home. You sit right down here and wait while I go finish what we came to do, then we'll go home."

"Are you coming back for me this time?" he demanded impatiently, sounding for the world like a spoiled little boy. "You didn't come back earlier, you know!"

"I just stepped in to check on Grandpa and Sadie and I completely forgot the time," she apologized sheepishly. "Would you like a soda pop or a candy bar while you wait? There's a vending machine down the hallway. I can have the nurse bring you something—"

"You keep *her* away from me," he cut in sharply.

"All right. All right! I'll hurry," she promised quickly.

Placing a quick kiss on his forehead, she left him sitting in the hallway staring blankly into space. She should have been more careful about the time. Just when she thought she was finally making progress with his paranoid fears of her profession, this had to happen!

158

Thirty minutes later she had both men safely loaded in the limousine and was on her way back home. One was feeling absolutely no pain, the other was sick to his stomach and extremely cranky, and *she* had a splitting headache!

CHAPTER NINE

It was growing very late when Taryn finished her work and slowly climbed the stairway back to her bedroom. The clock on the mantel was striking the hour of three as she yawned, then automatically began to unbutton her blouse as she entered her bedroom. Reed had disappeared the moment they arrived home. She had assumed he was going to bed, although he hadn't said where he was going. For one brief moment she hoped he had decided to sleep in her bed, then quickly berated herself for such thoughts. This madness between them had to stop.

The soft moonlight streaming through the window lit her pathway into her small bath as she shed the remainder of her clothes and slipped into the shower. Ten minutes later she turned off the bathroom light and rubbed moisturizer on her face as she walked over to the bed. She paused and smiled as she saw the strong masculine length of Reed burrowed under the light blanket. A strong arm came out to draw her under the cover as she slid willingly into the bed and cuddled against his warm body.

"Do you know it's three in the morning?" he asked in a drowsy voice.

"Yes, I think so. 'It's three in the mor-r-r-rn-n-ing,' " she sang dutifully, wrapping her arms around him and snuggling deeper against him.

"You feel good," he murmured, running his hands up her gown and gently massaging her cool bottom, "but you were absolutely right. Your voice stinks."

"Ummm . . . you feel good too," she acknowledged, fortifying her words with her eager hands. "And I never fib . . . well . . . almost never. What are you doing in my bed?"

"After the day I've put in, I wouldn't sleep in this house alone for love nor money," he stated flatly. "On top of that, I wanted to be with you. Any objections?"

"None, and I agree. You have had a horrible day," she granted with a tired sigh. "Maybe tomorrow will be better."

Neither one wanted to think about tomorrow as their mouths found each other and they kissed lazily, their tongues teasing and touching, then searching deeper, extracting the sweetness waiting therein. It occurred to Taryn that they both seemed perfectly happy to lie in each other's arms, seeking nothing more than the exquisite pleasure of being together. There was a sexual attraction neither one could deny, nor did they want to. But for the moment their needs went deeper than those of the flesh and they drifted

161

off to sleep in each other's arms kissing and holding one another tightly.

Early the next morning, the sound of birds singing woke Taryn up first. She lay for a moment trying to memorize Reed's handsome features, realizing that today could be the last they would spend together. In fulfilling her promise, Taryn had spoken with Ronnie and he had pledged to have the tree removed no later than noon today and would assess the damage. Reed had decided to borrow a car from the garage and the highways had been reopened late last night, so there would no longer be any reason for Reed to delay his departure.

She reached over and gently touched his hair. She loved the way it looked so tousled and boyish in his sleep. He was lying on his back, his arm slung over her chest. His mouth looked soft and so very kissable, she thought yearningly. There were tiny age lines beginning to form around his eyes, those beautiful silvery gray eyes that looked at her with such puzzlement at times, such unidentifiable longing at others. Her fingertip lightly traced the outline of his sleeping features, trying to indelibly score on her mind the man who had captured her heart in such a brief interval. Funny, there had only been two men in her life who had made love to her, and both had done so in a ridiculously short span of time. Soon Elaine would be lying in his arms, waking up to him every morning, accepting his kisses, having his children.

162

Elaine Montgomery. Mrs. Reed Montgomery. Tears rose up in Taryn's eyes. Mr. and Mrs. Reed Montgomery. Reed and Elaine Montgomery. Why was she doing this to herself? Wasn't it hard enough just lying here looking at him without torturing herself with things that were beyond her control?

The arm that had been lying on her chest closed slowly over her rib cage and brought her over against him. Turning on his side, he buried his face in her hair and whispered in a sleepy voice, "Hasn't anyone ever told you you can get in a lot of trouble looking at a man that way?"

Sure that her voice would betray her emotions, she could only shake her head and wipe hurriedly at the tears slipping down her cheeks. "I . . . I thought you were asleep."

"I was until a finger started running across my face," he murmured. "What time is it?"

"Close to six."

"Oh, good . . . too early to get up," he groaned, drawing her tighter into his embrace. His mouth began to search her neck languorously, nuzzling it in affection. "Don't you agree?"

"I never get up this early," she confessed. "In fact, I hate getting up mornings, period."

"You do? I do too." His mouth lazily captured hers. "Since we both hate getting up, let's just stay here for a while," he whispered persuasively. "I had great plans, but I fell asleep before I could proceed with them."

163

If she was any sort of decent person at all, this was where she should politely explain that what had occurred between them the night before was nice, and most likely unavoidable given the circumstances, but this was a new day and their madness must come to a halt. If she was to be fair to Elaine and not take advantage of a situation that was beyond Reed's or her control, she would force those words out of her mouth.

"Reed. Last night," she began.

"Did I happen to mention what great legs you have?" he asked softly, rubbing his hands along the silky texture of her thighs.

"Reed, about last night," she tried again, shivering as the hand moved to the inside of the silky softness and stroked suggestively.

"They are, you know. I'd like to see you in a bikini . . . one of those little skimpy things that barely leaves anything to a man's imagination." His voice was deep and hypnotic as his hands roamed over her in a tantalizing search of her pleasure points. "Do you have one of those?"

"I have a nice, serviceable one-piece," she returned, trying to keep her mind on business. "Reed, about last night. It was wonderful—"

"I agree. It was more than wonderful." He began to ravish her mouth with persistent kisses. "You already know how your hair turns me on, and your eyes, and the taste of your skin, and the sound of your voice when you whisper my name. Whisper my name again, Taryn," he ordered softly.

"Reed," she whispered, not in answer to his request, but out of her own need to get his attention.

"You say it so right. I've never heard a woman say it the way you do, all soft and breathless." His hands had found her full breasts and he paused to kiss each one thoroughly and lovingly, cradling their softness with such gentleness that it took her breath away.

"We shouldn't," she protested as she fervently returned his kisses now, her fingers threading through the dark waves of hair and pulling his mouth tighter against hers. "This has to stop, Reed."

"No, it doesn't," he murmured, moving his large body possessively over hers. "Don't spoil things, Taryn," he begged in a husky voice, showering hungry kisses along her eyes and jawline. "Let me love you . . . not just make love to you . . . let me share what's in my heart right now. I love you, don't you realize that by now? I know it's crazy and unexplainable and I haven't the slightest idea what we're going to do about it, but I love you."

The joy in her heart was so great she thought it would burst as she recognized the truth in his words. "I love you too, Reed."

"Honest?" He lifted his gaze to meet hers, a look of awe shimmering in his passion-laden gray depths. "I know you loved Gary and you're probably not over him yet, but would it ever be possible for another man to take his place in your heart?"

"No, you could never take his place," she confessed in a voice so filled with love he couldn't help but believe what she was about to say. "You'll have a place all your own."

"I've . . . I've never been in love before," he admitted, fingering a lock of her softly perfumed hair. "It feels strange to love someone so damn much it hurts."

"Don't you love your family?"

"Sure, but it's not the same. I haven't seen Mom and my three sisters for a while. Just wait until you meet them, honey, they're going to love you as much as I do . . ." His voice faltered and his eyes grew troubled as he realized what he had said. "Taryn . . . dear God, what am I going to do?" he murmured in a defeated voice.

"You're going to make love to me," she answered simply and honestly.

His thumbs grazed along the outline of her lips as he smiled, his eyes darkened to a smoldering gray. "We're going to make love to each other," he corrected. His mouth nudged hers open, tasting it, exploring it, then closing over it.

The feel of his hair-roughened chest pressed against the sensitive warmth of her bareness sent erotic sensations tumbling through her as she arched closer to his long, hard, powerful body. He deepened the kiss, his tongue tantalizing, demanding the response she so freely gave now.

"We were made for each other," he whispered, his

voice husky with passion. "Can't you feel how perfectly we fit together?"

Her answer was lost in Reed's groan of pleasure as his hands slid under her thighs and he lifted her body up to merge with his in searing, blinding pleasure.

Their lovemaking was urgent and fiery, tender and gentle, hungry and unquenchable, then slowed so they could take their time, drawing out the exquisite pleasures they were bringing to each other. Soft murmurs of gratification were muffled by long, agonizingly sweet kisses until they finally exploded into a single fireball, shattering out into the universe in a wondrous blaze of glory.

"Taryn, Taryn, my sweet, sweet Redhead," Reed whispered, kissing her over and over again as they floated slowly back to earth.

A soft weakness had invaded her bones now as she lay in his arms, showering his face with soft kisses. She didn't want to talk now, she didn't even want to think, she only wanted to lie in his embrace and feel his warmth against hers. His earlier words came back to drift meaningfully through her drowsy state. He had said it felt strange to love someone until it actually hurt. Well, she was feeling that "hurt" right now. So badly that she wanted to throw him in a shopping bag and run away with him somewhere where Elaine could never find him.

The sound of his soft breathing told her he was sleeping once more, as she drew the blanket back over them and cradled his head closer to her breast.

Her arms wrapped around Reed's neck more tightly as she stole one final kiss from his slack mouth, and snuggled back down in her pillow for another couple of hours sleep.

The air was strained later that morning as Reed and Taryn sat in the sunny breakfast nook eating their breakfast. Ronnie had knocked on the door ten minutes earlier and informed them the tree had been removed and that Reed's car was at the garage and the borrowed car was ready to go.

The subject of his imminent departure had not been broached, yet both knew the time was drawing near.

"More coffee?"

"No, thanks." Reed lit a cigarette and picked up the paper, glancing through it. "Boy, this thing's loaded with information," he mused. "Listen to this. 'Althea Burch and her daughter, Trealla, spent the afternoon shopping in Meadorville the day the storm hit. Trealla was purchasing her dress for the spring dance that was to be held this Friday evening in the Meadorville High gymnasium. Due to storm damages, the dance will now be held in the basement of the Legion Hall. Althea, along with Myrtle Mosely and Alice Woody, will be chaperoning the gala affair.'" He laid the paper down and gave Taryn a sexy wink. "Now that's one 'gala affair' I hate to miss."

Plucking the cigarette out of his mouth, she ground it out and pitched it in the wastebasket amid grunts of protest from him. "Stop making fun of our newspaper," she chided. "Where else can you get that sort of earthshaking news for fifteen cents?"

"Fifteen cents? Are you serious?" He picked up the paper again to examine the price and found that she was right. "I didn't think such bargains existed in the world today."

"There's a lot of things in this world you're not aware of," she said curtly. Now she had done it! She had been determined not to bring up any personal subject concerning her and Reed. If he had something to say, she wanted him to say it on his own, without any encouragement from her.

His face softened and he reached over and took her hand. "That may be, but I've learned a couple of things in the last few days that I wasn't aware of before."

Taryn drew her hand away from his, somehow sensing his next words. "You really are going to leave this morning, aren't you?" she asked softly.

"Taryn, don't look at me that way. You know I have to, don't you?" he prodded gently.

"Yes," she replied, forcing her gaze painfully away from his.

"I can't just ignore what's waiting for me in Santa Fe. What kind of person would I be to leave a woman standing at the altar?" His troubled eyes pleaded with hers for understanding.

"I'm aware of that, but I can't stand to think of you marrying someone you don't really love. . . . Oh,

169

Reed, don't you see that you'll be hurting Elaine as much as yourself if you step into a marriage bred of convenience?"

"Taryn . . . don't. Don't upset yourself. . . ."

"Don't upset myself!" She sprang to her feet in anger. "Don't you upset me! If you must go, then go! Don't stay around and torture me with trivial mishmash over what your duties to Elaine are!" Her face was flushed and angry as she faced him defiantly.

"I was afraid this would happen." Reed groaned and buried his hands in his hair in exasperation. "Can't you see I'm between the devil and the deep blue sea? What do you want me to do, Taryn? Pick up the phone and tell Elaine to 'dump her punch' because on the way to *our* wedding four days ago I found a redheaded mortician I've fallen crazy in love with? She wouldn't believe that in a million years!"

"Yes, that's exactly what I want!"

"No!" They glared at each other belligerently. "I won't do it that way. I'll have to go to her . . ."

Taryn didn't wait to hear him finish the sentence. She turned on her heel and marched toward the front parlor, muttering something under her breath.

"Stop grumbling, darn it!" Reed bellowed, helplessly trailing her through the house. "If you want to talk, say it so I can hear it!"

"Believe me, you wouldn't want to hear it," she yelled, tossing her red hair in defiance.

"Taryn, stop this nonsense and come back here. I want to talk to you—"

The loud slam of a door cut off his brusque demand. He glanced up and groaned in despair again. She had disappeared into Parlor B!

"Come out here, right now!" he ordered curtly through the closed door.

"You come in here if you want to talk to me" came her sharp, muffled reply. He could tell by her voice she was crying.

Mumbling obscenities under his breath, he hesitantly pushed the door open a crack and peered into the cool interior of the slumber room where Ralph Morliss lay reposing.

"Get out here!" he ordered.

"No!" She continued to arrange a spray of red roses, calmly ignoring him.

"You know I'm not coming in there. Get your fanny out here now!"

"No. Good-bye, Mr. Montgomery. Be sure and give Elaine my fondest regards!"

"I am going to get my car, then I'm leaving. Are you going to come out here and discuss this in a civilized manner or not?" His voice held grim authority now.

"Not," she answered crossly.

"Then I'm leaving!" He turned on his heel and started away, then whirled back around once more and opened the door a crack. "Don't forget to feed the damn bird!"

The door slammed closed again and she heard him march away in disgust.

Reed was gone by the time she came out of the parlor five minutes later. Her heart ached that their parting had to be so stormy, but she couldn't stand the pain of saying good-bye. He had certainly fooled her. After last night and his ardent confession of love, she could have sworn he *was* ready to tell Elaine to "dump her punch" or whatever. Men! Her eyes turned accusingly upward. "Men!" she reiterated aloud testily.

She forced herself to go into the office and try to concentrate on some forms that needed her attention. Her mind kept drifting back to Reed and Elaine and she began to simmer. It was simply not fair! He loved her, not Elaine! Why should she give up so easily and let another woman have him? Granted, Elaine had nabbed him first, but she should have made him love her enough that *nothing* could interfere with that love.

Taryn threw the pen she was using down on the desk and stood up, a call to arms resounding in her head. She had to stop Reed from leaving town! All she needed was a little more time to convince him of his madness.

Hanging a GONE TO LUNCH sign on the front door, she raced out the back, grabbing a set of keys on the way out. She noted with disgust that they were the keys to the hearse and knew Grandpa would skin her alive for taking it, but this was surely considered an emergency in anyone's books.

The big limousine was cumbersome to back out of

the drive, nevertheless she managed and was soon speeding down the road in front of the funeral parlor, plotting her devious course of action. She spotted Reed driving a car that was pulling into the street a few blocks ahead of her. Pushing down harder on the accelerator, she gained momentum on his vehicle and shot past him, waving happily at his surprised glance in her direction.

Minutes later the black hearse was idling smoothly in front of Reed's borrowed car as they sat at the stoplight waiting for the red light to change.

Reed had chosen to ignore her, aloofly turning his head away as she peered in the rearview mirror, innocently waving at him.

Good! There was Pryor, the town sheriff, sitting opposite her at the stoplight. This was going to work out splendidly, she congratulated herself as she raced the motor a fraction and slipped the transmission into reverse. This was going to cost her a pretty penny, but it was going to be worth it.

The light changed to green and she waved brightly to Pryor as he passed. When he was safely by, she stomped her foot down on the accelerator and prayed her grandpa wouldn't find out about this. The black car shot backward and a loud crunching sound filled the air as she came to a sudden halt, the back of the hearse buried in the borrowed car's grill.

Bounding hurriedly out of the car, she put on a sober face and marched over to where Reed was standing, angrily surveying the spewing radiator.

"What in the hell do you think you're doing!" he shouted, slamming his hands on his hips in agitation.

"Me! What do you think you're doing! You rear-ended me!" she accused hotly.

"Me! Are you crazy! I wasn't even aware the light had changed!"

"Well, of all the nerve. You hit me from behind and then try to stand here and tell me I am responsible. Well, this is unbelievable," she sputtered.

"I don't know what you're trying to pull, but you're not going to get away with it," Reed announced flatly, grimly surveying his mangled bumper and gaping radiator. "You hit me!"

"Here comes Pryor. We'll let him decide," she declared calmly.

"We certainly will!" Reed agreed.

The sheriff's car pulled up behind the two vehicles and Pryor got out, ambling slowly over to the scene of the accident. "Morning, Ms. Taryn," he greeted politely.

"Good morning, Pryor," she returned angelically. "I'm afraid Mr. Montgomery hit me in the rear."

"I'm going to stomp your rear if you don't stop lying!" Reed interjected swiftly. "Officer, this redheaded lunatic backed into me while we were sitting at that stoplight!"

"Backed into you, huh?" Pryor rubbed his jaw and solemnly contemplated the wrecked vehicles. "Backed into you, you say?" His voice sounded doubtful.

174

"That's right," Reed agreed with an earnest nod of his head. "I was sitting here minding my own business when all of a sudden she came flying back and took the whole front end out of the car."

"Honestly, Reed." Taryn placed her hands on her hips and looked at Pryor tolerantly. "Now, think, Pryor. Why in heaven's name would I be *backing* up at a stoplight? Don't you think that sounds like a desperate man who's trying to get out of a ticket?"

Pryor glanced from one opponent to the other. "Seems like that, don't it?" He took off his ten-gallon hat and scratched his head in puzzlement. "Nope, don't believe anyone would be backing up at a stopsign," he agreed reluctantly.

"Hey, you two!" Reed crossed his arms stubbornly. "I happen to be a lawyer and I will personally see you in court if you try to pull this on me! She hit me!" he flared in exasperation.

"Well." Pryor dragged out his ticket pad and started writing. "I'll be there. Just let me know when you're comin'."

"Taryn!" Reed's mouth dropped open and his arms sagged weakly back to his side as he realized he was about to be ticketed for something he didn't do. "I'm going to pop him in the mouth, you crazy woman! Tell him the truth!"

"Can you add, 'threatening an officer of the law' to that offense?" she asked Pryor helpfully.

"I'm being framed!" Reed shouted in disbelief as a

ticket was ripped off the pad and slapped firmly in his hand.

"Thirty dollars, or thirty days!" Pryor said flatly.

"I don't believe this!" Reed shouted as the sound of a horn broke into the heated discussion. Pryor, Reed, and Taryn glanced up to see a late-model convertible pulling up to the curb.

"Oh, brother! That's all I need," Reed groaned, slumping against the car.

"Reed, who is she?" Taryn asked, her voice growing fearful as she stepped closer to him and surveyed the pretty woman climbing out of the convertible and running toward the accident. Her heart grew numb as she awaited the inevitable, distressing answer.

"It's Elaine . . . and her mother," he confirmed tightly.

Moments later Elaine was throwing her arms around Reed and showering his face with kisses as she inquired whether he was hurt or not.

"Darling, Mother decided we should drive down and pick you up ourselves. We've had a heck of a time. We only knew the name of the town, but a nice man at the service station told us where your car had been trapped by the tree, but it was gone when we got there . . . it's just luck we noticed the accident here at the stoplight," Elaine explained, fussing with his windblown hair. "Are you all right? I've been so worried!"

Taryn didn't wait to hear Reed's comment as she

turned away from the painful scene, holding the tears back until she could make her way to the car. Elaine was here. She was real, and Taryn could no longer pretend she didn't exist. She was here, kissing the face that Taryn loved so very much . . . and she was pretty . . . very, very pretty.

"Ms. Taryn, do you need any help getting home?" Pryor shouted, surprised at her abrupt departure. "We need to fill out a report. . . ."

"Later," she called. "I'll stop by the office later. . . ."

Her hands trembled violently as she tried to start the hearse, feeling as if she was going to be sick any minute.

"Taryn!" She could hear Reed shouting to her as her motor sprang into life and she put the car in gear.

He suddenly appeared at the window, reaching in to still her hands, his gray eyes filled with such desolation that it only made her cry harder.

"Don't, Taryn, please don't do this," he pleaded huskily. "Give me time . . . I'll try to work this thing out . . ." he promised, tears forming in his eyes now too.

"Let me go, Reed. I don't think I can stand this. . . ." She took great gulping sobs of air as she tried to make her words come out intelligently. She had to get away from him before she broke down completely.

"Look at me, Taryn, are you all right?" His hand

tightened in concern as he brought her face force-fully up to meet his.

His fingers brushed hers, sending a sharp electrical current between them as she made herself look at him one last time. His face was tense, the tired lines around his eyes etched deeper than she remembered. For one crazy moment, she thought about kissing those lines away, trying to ease the pain she saw written on his face.

"Don't do this," he whispered in a barely audible voice. "I love you, Taryn."

Taryn swallowed her pride and grabbed his hand, burying her face in its familiar warm scent. "Don't go with her, Reed. I'll be anything you want me to be! I'll be the other woman if that's what it takes. I'll share you with her if that's what it takes to keep you, because I love you so very much and I don't think I can stand losing you." She broke down sobbing heart-brokenly.

"No, don't, sweetheart." His hand tightened pos-sessively on hers as Elaine's voice called impatiently to him.

Taryn turned tear-filled eyes up to meet his tor-tured gaze. "I'll give up being a mortician. I'll be anything in the world you want me to be if only you won't leave me." She had no idea where her pride had flown, but suddenly she was willing to offer any-thing if she didn't have to suffer this horrible loss.

He was so moved by her words, he could no longer

speak as Elaine's voice called out sharply again, "Reed! Are you coming?"

"You don't have to change, Taryn. You're everything in the world I want." He turned and strode away from the car, wiping self-consciously at his eyes with the sleeve of his jacket before Taryn could offer one final plea.

She sat for a moment pondering his words deep in her heart. She was everything he wanted. That's what he had said! The thought lifted her heavy burden. "God?" she called softly, turning her eyes toward the heavens. "Was he really telling me the truth or was he just trying to make things easier for me?" She thought for a minute and suddenly her spirits felt noticeably lighter. He'd sounded sincere! She frowned. Yet, if that were true, why was he getting into the car with the woman he was supposed to marry in four days? Her eyes shot upward once more. "I hope you have got this thing firmly in hand, because I've definitely lost control!" she conceded.

She drove away before she started crying again as Reed helped Pryor shove the damaged car over to the curb, then joined Elaine and her mother.

CHAPTER TEN

It was all over. Reed Montgomery and Elaine Matthews were married. It was late Saturday afternoon as Taryn climbed the small hill overlooking the cemetery and set Malcolm's birdcage down under the giant oak tree. The emerald-green leaves rustled pleasantly in the light breeze as she stood gazing over the lush countryside trying to will her mind to accept that fact. After all was said and done, he'd still gone ahead and married a woman he didn't love.

"He'll regret it," she told the bird solemnly.

Malcolm swung back and forth on his perch dejectedly. He had been unusually quiet the last few days. Taryn supposed he missed Sadie. Her stay in the hospital had been extended and she wouldn't be home until Monday.

She sighed and sat down on the ground next to his cage and idly offered him a Fig Newton, which he promptly refused. Having missed a few meals herself lately, she shrugged and bit into the cookie.

"He will, you know," she continued, chewing absently on the gooey filling. "One of these days Reed will wake up and look around and realize what a horrible mistake he's made."

"Squawk, Reed's a baaad boy. Reed's a baaad boy!" Malcolm confirmed.

"No, he isn't," Taryn said curtly, forgetting for a moment she was conversing with a bird. "Reed's wonderful. Don't talk badly about him. At first I had hard feelings toward him too. I thought he should have been wise and brave enough to stand up for what he wanted, but when you stop to think about it, Malcolm, that would have been an awful lot to ask of a person. It was very hard for me to trust my heart and admit that I could fall in love in three short days, so I can see what an impossible situation he found himself in. You know, Elaine planning a big wedding and all. And her father expecting him to be a part of his firm. I can see that," she confessed, glumly taking another bite of cookie. "Now, be honest. Can't you?"

Malcolm continued swinging, offering no comment to her question.

She sat watching the workman remove the canvas awning spread over the new grave site where they had laid Ralph to rest this afternoon. Unlike Martha's, the service had been peaceful and reverent. Reed would have liked that, she pondered sadly. No, he wouldn't, she corrected truthfully. He would have hated every minute and his allergy would have bothered him.

Tonight would be his wedding night. The cookie

turned to sawdust in her mouth as she stood up and angrily flung the remains over the hillsides.

"Oh, God." The pain closed in on her and made her cry out in exasperation. "Make him come driving up right now and tell me it's all over, that he told Elaine he couldn't possibly marry her because he's in love with *me* and we're going to get married and buy a chicken ranch and have lots of children and live happily ever after . . ." Her voice trailed off brokenly as she heard a car pull in the cemetery and stop. She squinted against the sun, trying to make out who the new arrival was. Her hazel eyes slowly grew round as dinner plates as she saw Reed's tall form climbing out of a new car. Her hand went over her mouth in disbelief, her eyes turning sheepishly toward the heavens. "Gosh," she breathed in a voice filled with reverence. "I was beginning to think you weren't listening!"

Reed glanced up toward the hillside and saw her standing there. His smile was warm, yet it contained a certain sternness as he placed his hands on his hips and shouted, "Are you ready to tell the truth about backing into me yet?"

"Uh . . ." She was having a horrible time finding her voice, hardly daring to believe he was actually standing down there shouting at her! "You . . . ran into me . . . I think," she called back nervously. What was he doing here? Oh, Lord. Surely he and Elaine hadn't stopped by on their honeymoon!

"Oh, no, I didn't!" he stated adamantly. He began

to make his way up the hillside as she sought to find some air for her lungs. "Thirty bucks, lady. That little fib cost you thirty bucks, plus the repair bill on the car that the garage loaned me." He reached the top of the hill with one hand waving a bill in front of her startled face. "What do you have to say in defense of your despicable actions?" he asked her in a stern voice.

"You . . . you're not wearing a wedding band," she noted hopefully.

Reed glanced down at the empty third finger of his left hand. "No, you haven't given me one yet. Now, back to problem number one. Why in the hell did you tear the whole front end out of that car!"

"You didn't marry Elaine this afternoon?" she pursued, her voice lifting slightly with the first faint rays of hope.

"No, I can't marry Elaine. I'm in love with you."

"Just like that. You're in love with me?"

"Well, not just like that. It took four whole days," he told her solemnly. "Now, why did you back into me?"

"Because I didn't want you to leave. Was she upset?"

"Wouldn't it have been simpler and a lot less costly just to ask me not to leave? I planned on coming back," he said patiently. "If you had let me explain that day instead of running into that slumber room and hiding, I would have told you I planned on going to Santa Fe to explain to Elaine the best way I knew now what had happened, and to break the engagement. And, yes, she was a bit miffed. Don't plan on getting *her* business when she goes."

"You're not engaged anymore?"

"I didn't say that."

"You didn't break the engagement?" Her face fell as hard as her hopes.

"I'm still engaged," he confirmed easily.

She frowned at him sullenly. "To whom?"

"To youwhom," he mispronounced teasingly.

Her frown softened. "To . . . me?"

"To you." He grinned. "Why do you find that so surprising? Isn't it perfectly natural for a man who hates the mere thought of cemeteries, ghosts, ghouls, Halloween, dogs howling at full moons, and witches —not to mention driving hearses, singing at funerals, and slinking around hospitals picking up dead bodies —to find himself stranded in a town with a redheaded mortician whom he falls head over heels in love with in three—actually I think it was closer to two—days? He's willing to give up a lucrative law practice making a staggering amount of money each year, to leave a lovely woman whom he's been friends with for as long as he can remember stranded at the church altar with her punch already made and in the bowl waiting for the seven hundred guests the bride and groom have invited. He throws *all* that away without so much as a second thought and races back here in a new car he just drove out of the showroom to plead with this lovely mortician to marry him. What's so strange about that?" he asked calmly.

"Oh," she scoffed weakly, "Elaine didn't really have her punch made and she wasn't actually standing at the altar . . . was she?" Taryn would have felt terrible if Reed had been that callous. The price of ingredients for punch was sky-high nowadays! she agonized, her practical side surfacing now.

"Squawk! Reed's a baaad boy! Squawk, Reed's a baaad boy." Malcolm had suddenly decided to voice his opinion.

"Shut up, Malcolm, this is between me and the lady," he advised the bird sternly. "No, it hadn't quite reached that point yet," Reed continued, reaching out to hesitantly touch the strands of her titian hair ruffling gently in the spring breeze. "I'll bet you thought I wasn't coming back, didn't you, Red?"

She nodded, her eyes devouring his familiar features lovingly. "Pinch me," she demanded softly.

He reached out and tenderly pinched the end of her nose.

"I felt that!" Her smile was radiant as the tips of her trembling fingers ran adoringly over the hollows and planes of his face, drinking in his unique scent, the feel of his skin against hers. "I'm not dreaming, am I? You're here, you're real. . . ."

"I'm here, and I'm real." Their gazes caught and held silently for a moment, both so overcome with emotion for the moment, they couldn't speak.

"I'm sorry I took so long in coming back, but I couldn't leave Elaine alone to face all the things that had to be done to cancel the wedding," he apologized, sensuously stroking the corners of her mouth with his thumbs. "I know I should have called to tell you that I had broken the engagement, but I wanted you in my arms when I told you."

"Oh, Reed," she sighed, drowning in her happiness yet acutely feeling Elaine's pain. "Was she very . . . hurt?"

The gray of his eyes clouded for the briefest of moments. "I can't say that it was easy on either one of us, Taryn. True, I wasn't in love with Elaine, but I do admire and respect her and her parents."

"When did you tell her?"

"The day she came to get me. When we arrived in Santa Fe, we went straight to her parents' home and that's when I broke the news to all of them. They were very polite and I think her parents just might have understood, but I'm afraid it didn't ease Elaine's pain . . . or humiliation. In any other circumstances, I would have never done that sort of thing to anyone . . . but through it all I kept remembering what you had said to me once. You said, there comes a time for people when they have to decide how they want to live their lives, and with whom. Do you know I had never candidly stopped to ask myself that question? I had always sort of flowed along with the tide, taking each day as it came and never really thinking about the future or what I wanted? Until I made love

186

to you and felt that overpowering need to have you beside me for the rest of my life, I continued to ignore what I wanted. It was just easier to please everyone else." His eyes darkened to a passionate slate gray as he surveyed the lovely features he had seen over and over in his dreams the last four nights. "But once I held you in my arms and experienced how wonderful love—not like—could be, of the joy you could bring into my life, I was forced to ask the question and come up with the only possible answer. I love you, redheaded Taryn Oliver. Today, tomorrow, next year, forever after . . . and *in* the forever after, if you'll let me."

They shifted nearer to each other, their mouths moving closer and closer together as they talked. Taryn was dying for him to kiss her, but he seemed willing to let his eyes express his feelings for the moment, love radiating out of their smoky depths.

"Are you ready to let me take care of you from now on?" he asked in a hopeful voice, his breath gently caressing her cheeks as he touched his face to hers. "I know you'll never forget Gary, but I promise to love you as much or more than he did."

"Oh, darling, of course I'll never forget Gary, and no matter what you think, I have put him in his rightful place, Reed. You're all I ever have or ever will want.

"Reed," she murmured, snuggling closer to his broad chest. "When are you going to kiss me?"

"Not until I can't stand it another second, which

isn't far away," he confirmed, avoiding her tempting mouth that was clearly aching to be kissed. "Once I start kissing you, I won't be stopping for a while and we still have things to be decided."

"Did you kiss Elaine good-bye?" she asked, wishing she hadn't.

Reed's grin was defiantly guilty. "One kiss," he defended. "Surely you're not going to be jealous over one kiss out of the fifty million I plan on giving you in the next couple of hours alone!"

"I certainly *am* jealous, and that had better be the last time you ever kiss another woman, or you're a dead duck, Reed Montgomery," she stated adamantly.

He flinched painfully. "Dead duck. That brings us to the next problem that needs to be discussed."

"Such as?" she asked with disappointment, refusing to relinquish her tight hold around his neck.

"Such as, were you serious about living anywhere with the man you loved?"

"Indubitably, dear! Where do you want to live?"

"Well, there is this beautiful piece of land about twenty miles from here. I noticed it on the way out of town the other day. . . ."

"You mean the land out by the new highway . . . the one that has the lovely old two-story house that sits back in the woods?"

"Yeah! You know the one I'm talking about?" he asked excitedly. "The one with all the white fences surrounding the land?"

"Yes! I love the place myself! I called the realtor yesterday and it's priced very reasonably," she assured.

"You called about it? Why?"

Taryn's grip around his neck increased. "Well, I was thinking if my prayers were answered and you *did* come back, the land would make a lovely chicken ranch."

"You did! That's exactly what *I* was thinking!" He picked her up in his arms and swung her around and around, both of them laughing with delight.

"You would really give up being a mortician and live on a chicken ranch with me?" he asked happily.

"I'd *be* a chicken for you, if that's what you wanted!" she exclaimed, hugging him with exuberance. "But what about you? Do you honestly want to give up being a lawyer after all the hard years you've spent in law school?"

"I really don't think either one of us has to give up our profession," he replied, with a broad grin. "Surely Meadorville, population six hundred and forty-three, can up their total by one more and have room for a small law office in their sprawling metropolis. Then in the evenings I can come home to you and we can have our chickens until our children come along. In the meantime, you can still help your grandfather with his . . . business." He paused and squeezed her with authority. "As long as you don't involve me in any of your emergencies. I love you, but there's a limit to what my nerves can take!"

189

"Oh, I won't ever ask you to help me again," she promised, bringing her mouth closer to his once more. "Can we kiss now?"

He cocked his head and smiled at her wickedly. "Can't wait, huh?"

"Reed . . . kiss me!"

"Not yet," he procrastinated, enjoying the look of childlike disappointment covering her face. He walked over to the birdcage and leaned down. "Are you feeling any better about yourself yet, fella? What you need is a good woman to set your feathers on fire. Maybe a redheaded one like I have," he suggested helpfully, handing the bird a Fig Newton.

Turning back to Taryn, he smiled and held out his arms in warm welcome. "And now I would be more than happy to give you that kiss . . . and a hundred more besides. Come here, Redhead, and let's show him what can happen to a guy when he falls in love."

Taryn flew into his arms and they kissed hungrily, their hands exploring and touching each other with fervor. The kisses were sweet, then demanding, then poignant, both pouring out their love for the other, both finding it hard to believe that they were together once more, this time never to be parted again.

"Squawk! Reed *is* baaad boy!" Malcolm reminded primly as Reed's hand slipped beneath her blouse and lovingly caressed her feminine softness.

"You don't know the half of it, Malcolm," he chuckled wickedly as Taryn's face blushed a rosy pink. His hands intimately began to take possession of every

190

inch of her silken skin as he drew her closer in his arms. "Before I take you home and make love to you until *your* feathers burn, there's one more thing I'd like to do," he whispered suggestively.

"Anything," she offered devotedly.

Reed affected a low, gentlemanly bow. "I would like to have the honor of dancing with my best girl." He held out his arm politely. "Milady. If I might?"

Taryn curtsied and demurely accepted his hand.

Reed turned and bowed again to Malcolm. "Sir, you will join us?" He picked up the birdcage and winked at Taryn sexily. "I hope you don't mind, but you know how sensitive he can be."

"I quite understand," she returned with formal consent.

Holding the birdcage with one finger, he placed his large hands lightly in hers and they began to slowly waltz under the spreading oak, their gazes locked adoringly. Amid the rustle of the leaves, he began to sing to her, his beautiful baritone voice ringing out loud and clear over the quiet hillside. To the melody of "Let Me Call You Sweetheart," he whirled her and Malcolm around the grassy meadow as the birds in the trees twittered noisily in sweet accompaniment.

There were a few parts in the song he improvised, making up his own words to tell her of his love. Taryn found herself giggling, then flushing bright red at times with his racy lyrics, but she thought it was the most lovely dance she had ever had.

When their feet finally slowed, they came together in a long, smoldering kiss as Malcolm settled down contentedly to swing back and forth on his perch, enjoying his Fig Newton for the first time in a week.

"Take me home, Taryn." Reed raggedly made the familiar plea against the sweetness of her mouth as she drew him closer to her heart.

"Yes, darling. And, this time, I will keep you."

As he buried his face in the perfume of the hair he loved so very much, she turned her eyes once more toward the blue of the heavens. Making a perfect round circle with her thumb and forefinger, she lifted the salute gratefully as her mouth silently formed the words *Thanks!*